Too Proud To Beg

Juanita turned and looked at Stone. "Tell Rodrigo you are sorry, señor. Get down on your knees and beg him for your life. That is your only chance, because he is going to kill you."

"Do as he says," Stone said to her. "Get out of the way before you get hurt."

"This is my fault," Juanita said. "I should never have spoken with you, gringo. Your death will be a stain on my soul forever."

"Move," Stone told her softly.

She stepped back into the crowd, and near her Stone saw Lobo the Apache.

"Go for his belly," Lobo said. "Remember who you are."

WARPATH

Josh Edwards

DIAMOND BOOKS, NEW YORK

WARPATH

A Diamond book / published by arrangement
with the author

PRINTING HISTORY
Diamond edition / May 1991

ISBN: 1-55773-513-1

Diamond Books are published by The Berkley Publishing
Group, 200 Madison Avenue, New York, New York 10016.
The name "Diamond" and its logo are trademarks
belonging to Charter Communications, Inc.

PRINTED IN THE UNITED STATES OF AMERICA

10 9 8 7 6 5 4 3 2 1

WARPATH

1

THE DESERT LAY vast and golden below him, gleaming in the bright sunlight. There were trees and clumps of grass, cactuses and large rocks, but mostly it was rolling hills of sand all the way to the blue mountains in the distant haze.

It was hot as hell, and John Stone took off his old Confederate cavalry hat, wiping his forehead with the back of his arm, his dark blond hair gleaming in the sunlight. He was from South Carolina, and it was nothing like this.

This took away his energy and made him dizzy. When he breathed, it was like breathing the air in a furnace. Somehow the Apaches made their life here. This was the Apache homeland.

Their fierce spirit was the last touch in this desert inferno. And they just didn't shoot you and let it go at that; they might set fire to you, skin you alive, stake you out on an anthill, use you for target practice, let their kids tear you apart with knives. They stopped you any way they could.

Stone held his spyglass to his eye and scanned the terrain back and forth. Ride to the next hill, climb it, and take another look—that was his method. He was making his way to Tucson, sleeping at night in the best hiding places he could find, lying down with the rattlers.

The folks in Nolan had advised him that Apaches had been seen in the area, and urged Stone not to go onto the desert, but Nolan hadn't been much of a town, and Stone knew he'd go crazy there.

Besides, he could handle himself. He'd been a cavalry officer during the Civil War, under Wade Hampton and Jeb Stuart. He'd seen five years of combat, and had been in the middle of some of the bloodiest battles in the history of the world.

He'd also been on the frontier for four years, and had fought Indians before. Once, on a wagon train, they'd been attacked by Comanches, and it had been as bad, and maybe worse, than the war. The Comanches had been ferocious, more like wild animals than men. The fight had been hand to hand, down and dirty, and there were many moments when Stone thought he wasn't going to make it.

The folks in Nolan told him that Apaches would make Comanches look like schoolchildren on a spree. His tactics were to proceed cautiously, stay off the main trails, and don't linger at water holes. He'd been entranced by a water hole in Texas once and got a Comanche arrow through his leg.

Movement in the distance caught his eye. Peering through the spyglass, he adjusted the focus, as beads of sweat dripped down his tanned cheeks and stubbled jaw, and the sun glinted off his burnished spurs.

Something definitely was out there among the sand devils and cottonwood trees—a large number of riders moving west in a column of twos.

A chill came over him, although the temperature was nearly one hundred degrees. He was hidden well, his horse behind him. If he stayed still, the Apaches couldn't see him. They weren't moving in his direction, and all he had to do was let them pass.

Then he saw blue among them, and realized they weren't Apaches at all. They were U.S. Cavalry. The corners of his mouth turned up in a smile.

He decided to ride with the cavalry to the next town, or wherever they were going. Arising, he carried his Henry rifle back to his horse. Stone was six feet two inches tall, with broad shoulders and thick muscles. His black boots were high-topped, and his jeans were tucked into them, cavalry style. He approached his big black horse and dropped the rifle into the boot. Then he mounted up and urged the horse down the hill toward the cavalry.

The horse half walked and half skidded down the side of the hill. Three vultures circled in the sky overhead, and a coyote howled mournfully in the distance.

He passed a scattered growth of juniper, prickly pear, pine oak, and ocotillo. Stone had to be careful where he guided his horse, because he didn't want him stabbed by the painful needles that were everywhere.

Apaches were only one lethal feature of the hostile desert environment. There were also wild cats, wild dogs, and bear, not to mention poisonous snakes, lizards, and insects. Death and pain lurked everywhere.

Stone's horse walked across the desert, and Stone reached for one of his canteens, unscrewed the lid, and raised it to his mouth, drinking sparingly. A bird flew to the red flower on the top of the saguaro cactus next to him, and Stone looked up at it.

The desert was dangerous, but also incredibly beautiful. There was an interesting variety of plants and animals, and the vistas were breathtaking. From certain viewpoints, he could see twenty miles of buttes, plateaus, and mesas, and the light was so intense it made the rainbow of colors exceptionally vivid.

It was heaven and hell combined. Reaching into his shirt pocket, he took out his bag of tobacco and rolled himself a cigarette. He struck the match on the side of his jeans and lit the end.

"Hold it right there," said a voice in front of him. "I got you in my sights, and if you try anythin' funny you're a dead man."

Stone pulled back on his horse's reins, and the horse perked up his ears, looking toward his right. A man with a white mustache, wearing buckskin and a curve-brimmed leather hat, came out from behind a clump of cactus, carrying a rifle in his hands. He was followed by an Apache Indian, and two Apaches emerged from the foliage on the other side of Stone.

"Who're you?" the man asked.

"John Stone."

"Where you headed?"

"Tucson."

The man narrowed his eyes as he peered up at Stone. "Just checkin' to make sure who you was. You're takin' a helluva chance, feller, ridin' across the desert in broad daylight like you are. If any Apaches'd been around, they woulda been on you like stink on shit."

"Aren't those Apaches there with you?"

"They work for the Army and so do I." The man pointed behind Stone. "We seen you on that hill back there."

Stone was surprised, because he'd thought he couldn't be seen back there. "How'd you do that?"

"Saw somethin' shinin' up there."

"Must've been my spyglass."

"Got to be careful with a spyglass. Sometimes it's safer not to use 'em at all." The man held up his hand. "I'm Tim Connors, cavalry scout."

"John Stone."

They shook hands, and Stone could feel the wiry strength in the old man's body. Stone figured he must be in his sixties, with deep wrinkles in his tanned face and a few of his teeth missing. The Apache scouts' faces were blank, red bandannas tied around their heads. Their skin was brown and their eyes were slitted.

"You might as well join up with us," said Connors. "Be safer that way."

"That's what I was intending to do. Where are you headed?"

"Fort Kimball. It's about ten miles thataway." Connors pointed toward the west.

"Is it near a town?"

"Santa Maria del Pueblo. We'll git our horses and be right with you."

Connors and the Apaches ran into the brush and returned a few moments later atop their horses. The Apaches went first, and Stone rode behind Connors, because there wasn't enough space to ride beside him. Connors was slim, around five feet eight inches tall, and the skin on the back of his neck looked like old Spanish leather.

They came to a wide trail, and Connors pulled back his reins, stopping in the middle of it. Stone looked west and saw a cloud of dust in the distance, the oncoming cavalry. Connors took a sip of water from his canteen. The Apaches scanned the surrounding countryside, and Stone could sense their strength and wildness. They reminded him of the Comanches in Texas.

"You lived out this way long?" Stone asked Connors.

"Thirty years, more or less."

Stone took a photograph out of his shirt pocket and handed it to him. "Ever see her?"

Connors looked at the photograph, covered with isinglass in a silver frame. It showed a pretty young blond woman in a high-necked dress. "Don't think so. Who is she?"

"Friend of mine."

Connors handed the photograph back, and Stone dropped it into his shirt pocket, buttoning the flap.

Connors looked at him disapprovingly. "You're not gonna last long out here, because you're not payin' attention. An Apache could be on top of you before you knew what hit you."

"I thought we were safe, now that the cavalry is close by."

"You're never safe on the desert, and never will be until ev'ry damn Apache is dead. Keep yer eyes open. Apaches ain't afraid of the cavalry."

Stone looked at the Apache scouts, who appraised him calmly. The coyote howled again in the distance, echoing across mesas and canyons. Vultures circled overhead, while the saguaro cactuses stood like sentinels.

"What about those Apaches you've got with you?" Stone asked. "Why are they working for the Army?"

"They do a job and git paid for it, same as me."

The cavalry column came closer, their flags and guidons fluttering in the air, with the usual cavalry racket of hoofbeats and jangling equipment. Stone closed his eyes for a few seconds, and it reminded him of the war.

Opening his eyes again, he saw the blue uniforms covered with dust and alkali. The men were hunched over, wilting in their saddles, but their commanding officer sat upright and raised his hand. The cavalry column stopped behind him.

"What've you got there, Connors?" asked the commanding officer, a young lieutenant with a clipped black mustache.

"Found this feller wanderin' around," Connors replied. "His name's John Stone."

Stone urged his horse forward until he was beside the officer. They shook hands.

"I'm Lieutenant Joshua Lowell," the officer said. "What're you doing?"

"Headed for Tucson."

"You must be new to this country, otherwise you wouldn't be traveling out here alone."

"As a matter of fact I am new to this area."

"It's not safe out here."

"I thought I could handle myself."

"You'd better ride with us to Fort Kimball."

Lieutenant Lowell raised his hand and then moved it forward. The cavalry soldiers advanced over the trail. Stone took his place beside Lieutenant Lowell, and estimated there were about sixty men in the troop. The sun shone like a pan of silver in the sky, and Stone felt beads of sweat roll down his cheek. Connors rode ahead with his Apache scouts, to check the terrain.

Lieutenant Lowell turned to Stone. "I see you're wearing an old Confederate cavalry hat. Were you in the war?"

"Yes."

"What unit?"

"First South Carolina Cavalry."

"See any action?"

"Enough."

"I regret that I was too young for the war, but other times I'm glad I missed it. It was quite a time, I imagine."

"Wouldn't want to go through it again," Stone replied.

"Some of the old-timers say it's worse out here in Apache country. This isn't normal warfare, where you face your enemy and fight him according to the book. Apaches never come straight at you like in the battles of the Civil War. They favor ambush and sneak attacks. You never know where they are, and for all we know, there might be a whole army of them watching us right now, ready to spring the trap."

Stone scanned the desert, looking for unusual movements

and shapes, but there were only scattered bushes, clumps of cactuses, and tall saguaros standing like human beings with their arms upraised. Ahead, the Apaches with Connors moved off the main trail.

"I didn't realize Apaches worked for the Army," Stone said. "I wonder why they betray their own people?"

"Money. Also, they have feuds among themselves, and this is the way some of them get back at the others."

"Aren't you worried that they might betray you too? I mean, if they're capable of betraying their own people, they might do the same to you."

"Hasn't happened yet."

Stone looked sideways at Lieutenant Lowell. "How long have you been out here?"

"A little over a year."

"Is it your first assignment?"

"How did you guess?"

"You're not that old. Did you go to West Point?"

"Yes. I take it you were an officer during the war?"

"I was."

"Did you go to the Point too?"

"The war broke out in my senior year, and I joined the Confederate Army."

"What brings you here?"

Stone unbuttoned his shirt pocket and handed him the photograph. "I'm looking for this woman. Ever see her?"

Lieutenant Lowell gazed at the photograph. "She's very pretty. Who is she?"

"Friend of mine."

"Don't believe I know the lady." Lieutenant Lowell returned the photograph. "What happened to her?"

"Don't know. That's why I'm looking for her." Stone dropped the picture into his pocket. "Have you ever fought the Apaches?"

"A few times. They're quite different from the Plains Indians, I'm told. The Plains Indians fight for glory and honor, but Apaches fight to kill, maim, terrorize, torture, and rape. If you ever see an Apache, you'd better kill him before he kills you."

"Except for your scouts."

"No, don't kill my scouts."

"They must be a hardy people to survive out here."

"There's nothing tougher than an Apache, and they know this land thoroughly. Fighting and raiding is their life. When they get old, they get left behind in the desert to die, because an Apache who can't fight is useless. The kids learn war as soon as they can walk, and some of their women are as deadly as the men. But the Apaches can't hold out forever. More settlers are moving to this territory every day. In another ten or twenty years the Apaches won't exist."

"It's a big country," Stone said. "There's a lot of room to hide."

"It's only a matter of time before they're wiped out. They're a primitive people, basically, and they won't be able to stop a modern army with modern weapons."

Stone glanced at Lieutenant Lowell, the handle of Lieutenant Lowell's cavalry saber glinting in the sun. Stone had carried a similar saber during the war, and cut down many soldiers in blue, like Lieutenant Lowell.

"Where are you from, Lieutenant?" Stone asked.

"Boston. How about you?"

"South Carolina, near Columbia."

Boston had been the heart of the abolition movement before the war, and South Carolina was plantation country. Stone's family had owned a large plantation with many slaves, but now he rode across the desert with an officer in blue from Boston. The world had turned upside down in only a few years.

Lieutenant Lowell turned to him, and his eyes were red-rimmed from the glaring sun. "Ever think of returning to the Army?"

"No thanks."

"It's a tough life, but I can't imagine anything better."

"I can."

"Such as what?"

"I'd like to have a ranch somewhere."

"If it weren't for the Army, there wouldn't be any ranches on the frontier."

"I've had enough war."

"The Apaches may have something to say about that."

"I wonder if any of them are around right now?"

"I don't think so, because if they were, they would've killed you."

Three figures lay flat on the ground atop the hill where Stone had lain with his spyglass.

One was Red Feather, the medicine man, and the other two were Black Bear and Eagle Claw. They'd been gathering plants and herbs for their ceremonies when they'd seen the lone rider on the black horse in the distance. Slowly they'd closed with him, to kill him, steal his horse and weapons, but then the bluecoats had arrived.

Now they watched their quarry riding away. They'd stalked him for three hours and had been close enough to see his fine horse and weapons. He'd been blundering across the desert like a fool, and it would've been easy to kill him, leaving his stripped corpse in the middle of the trail, to warn other white eyes that the desert still belonged to the Apaches.

The bluecoats rode off in the direction of Fort Kimball, and Red Feather needed a new rifle badly, because the one he had was worn out, often misfiring, and it was difficult to obtain ammunition.

In the old days, the bluecoats below him would have been wiped out in an ambush, a fast and ferocious slaughter, but now Apache traitors who worked for the bluecoats would detect the ambush before it was sprung, so bluecoats rode through Apache land as if they owned it, and the Apaches could do little to stop them.

Red Feather looked up at the sky and saw three vultures flying away. They'd been expecting to make a meal of the lone white rider, but the bluecoats had saved his life and the vultures would have to find another meal.

Red Feather watched the big white eyes on the black horse riding toward Fort Kimball with the soldiers. *You got away this time,* Red Feather thought, *but maybe next time you will not be so lucky.*

2

IT WAS NIGHT when the cavalry troop arrived in Santa Maria del Pueblo, and the streets were crowded with processions of Mexicans. Torches and lamps blazed in front of squat adobe buildings, and men wearing huge sombreros strummed guitars. Children, begging for coins, ran alongside the cavalry soldiers.

Stone rode in front of the column with Lieutenant Lowell and the scouts.

"The Mexicans're having their yearly festival here," Lieutenant Lowell explained, the light from lanterns flickering on his youthful face. "On this date, about seventy-five years ago, the Virgin Mary supposedly was seen here by a Franciscan priest. A church was built on the site where the visitation took place. People from miles around come here for the holiday every year."

"Where's the livery stable?"

"Just down the street on the right. The hotel's next door. The best restaurant in town is the La Briza, if you like spicy food. If you want to come out to the fort, just ask for me. We can have a drink together at the officers' club."

11

"I'll take you up on that one of these nights," Stone said. "Thanks for accompanying me here."

"Glad to have you along. Do yourself a favor and don't go out on the desert alone anymore."

Stone touched a finger to the brim of his hat and pulled his horse away from the cavalry troop. Stone's horse danced at the side of the road as the cavalry troop passed, clanging and pounding, sending up a cloud of dust. Stone rode into the livery stable and pulled the saddle off the black. He rubbed it down, as it ate oats in the trough.

Stone patted the horse on its massive haunch. "See you later, old boy. I've got to tie on the feed bag myself."

He tossed the saddlebags over his shoulder and walked to the sidewalk. A child ran by, blowing a tin horn, and a Mexican on a horse yipped and yelled as he rode toward the saloon at the end of the street. Stone came to the Cardenas Hotel, a sprawling adobe structure, and entered the lobby. American cowboys and Mexican men sat around on the chairs, talking loudly, and a Mexican with a long black mustache with the ends turned up worked behind the desk.

"Room for the night," Stone said, "in back where it's quiet."

"You are new in town, señor?"

"Just arrived."

"I am Pedro Cardenas, and this is my establishment. Welcome." He shook Stone's hand. "Where are you coming from?"

"Nolan."

"What brings you to Santa Maria del Pueblo?"

Stone took out the picture of Marie and showed it to him. "Ever see this woman?"

"She is very pretty, but no, I do not believe that I have. Who is she?"

"Friend of mine."

"Perhaps if you go to the church and pray to the Virgin, you will find her."

Stone signed the register and Pedro Cardenas gave him a key. Stone walked down a corridor lined on both sides with doors, and finally came to his room. He unlocked the door and walked inside, lighting the coal-oil lamp on the dresser with a match.

The room was a tiny cell containing a narrow cot, a wooden chair, and the dresser. A brightly colored Mexican blanket covered the cot, and Stone sat on it, rolling a cigarette. A crucifix hung on the wall above the bed.

This was the first time Stone ever had been in a town that was predominantly Mexican, and he felt as if he were in a foreign country. Puffing the cigarette, he took out the picture of Marie and looked at it. For four years he'd ridden from town to town on the frontier, showing her picture, and no one had seen her. Sometimes it got discouraging, but Stone kept at it. He couldn't forget her.

They'd grown up on neighboring plantations in South Carolina, and he'd loved her ever since he was a little boy. They became engaged while he was at West Point, and then the war came. When he returned home after Appomattox, the plantation had been burned to the ground, his parents had died, and Marie had disappeared. Nobody knew what happened to her. Some thought she'd gone west with a Union officer.

That had been difficult for Stone to believe, but all he could do was come west and look for her. He'd never worked a day in his life before going to West Point, but now he was just another drifter on the frontier, carrying another dream in his heart, the dream of a woman calling to him from the past and leading him into the future.

He thought he'd rest for a couple of days in Santa Maria del Pueblo and then move on to Tucson. Maybe he could travel with a stagecoach or other people, since everybody thought he shouldn't be out on the desert alone.

His stomach rumbled and he decided to get something to eat, but first he had to clean up. A basin and pitcher of water were on the dresser, and he washed his face and hands, then combed the dust and alkali out of his hair. He thought he ought to shave, because he had four days of stubble on his cheeks and chin, but thought he'd do that in the morning.

He put on a clean red shirt and tucked it into his pants, then readjusted his two crisscrossed gunbelts. He wore Colts in greased holsters tied to his legs.

He put on his old cavalry hat and smiled at himself in the mirror, and his white teeth gleamed in the light of the lamp. He left the hotel room and made his way through the network of corridors to the lobby and then the sidewalk outside.

Three señoritas walked by, their long skirts billowing around them. Stone passed a group of Mexican men in wide sombreros, blowing a lively Mexican tune on their trumpets. A skinny little Mexican boy with ragged clothes and big brown eyes ran up to Stone and tugged at his shirt.

"Fifty cents my sister," the boy said. "She is beautiful—you will like her."

"Sorry."

"Forty cents?"

Stone shook his head, but the boy wouldn't let him go.

"What is wrong with you, cowboy?" the boy asked mockingly. "Don't you like pretty girls?"

Stone stopped and looked down at him. "How can you sell your own sister?"

"For the money, cowboy. Come on, you pay now and have a good time, yes?"

"Afraid not."

"Thirty cents?"

Stone handed him a few coins. "You look like you could use a good meal."

The boy stopped and stared at the coins in his dirty palm, as if unable to believe what had happened. Stone continued to walk and came to a public square crowded with people. A small church with a tall spire was in the background, illuminated by torches. Vendors sold food at little wooden stands and a band was playing beside the church, while couples danced to the music.

The little boy caught up with Stone and looked up at him. "You are new in town, no?"

"Yes."

"I am Paco, and I will be your friend. Who are you?"

"My name's John Stone."

"I will show you everything. What do you want to see first?"

Stone stared at crowds of people entering and leaving the church, and recalled what Pedro Cardenas had said about praying for good luck in his search for Marie.

"Are you hungry?" Paco asked. "This man here sell very fine burritos."

Stone looked in the direction where Paco was pointing, and

saw a sad-faced Mexican at a wooden stand. "Get two," Stone said to Paco, dropping more coins into his hand.

Paco ran off to the vendor, and Stone stared at the church. It was crude, obviously slapped together by local citizens, a fortress of God in the middle of the desert. Some people laughed nearby, and seven Mexicans galloped past on horses, firing their pistols in the air.

Paco returned with two white rolls of dough, and handed one to Stone. "You will like it," he said. "It will make you strong with women."

Stone bit into the burrito, and it was like eating fire. Tears came to his eyes and he coughed.

"I get you something to drink!" Paco shouted.

The boy ran off, and Stone swallowed the food desperately. Nearby, an old gray-haired Mexican woman laughed at him.

"You gringos are ridiculous," she said.

"Food's pretty hot."

"It is not the food. You are weak, like all gringos. You do not know what is good, and you destroy everything you do not understand."

The old woman stepped back into the crowd, just as Paco broke through, carrying two glasses of beer, and handed one to Stone.

"Drink!" Paco commanded.

Stone raised the glass to his lips and took a swig. It was ice-cold. "How much do I owe you?"

"Fifty cents."

Stone handed him more coins, and Paco counted them carefully like a teller in a bank. Stone took another bite out of the burrito, and this time it didn't burn so much. It was filled with beans and meat with a special sauce.

"Where you want to go now, John Stone?" the boy asked, his mouth full of burrito.

"I think I'll go in that church over there, after I finish eating."

"You are Catholic?"

"No."

"What are you?"

"I don't know."

"Do you believe in God?"

"I think so."

"What do you believe in more than anything else in the world?"

Stone thought for a few moments, then tapped one of his Colt .45s. "This."

"They say that whatever you believe in more than anything else, that is your God."

"What do you believe in?"

"*Jesús Cristo.*"

"How can you believe in Jesus Christ, and then try to sell me your sister for fifty cents?"

"A man has got to eat."

"Don't you go to school?"

"My father says that in school you only learn to be *estúpido.*"

"Everybody needs an education."

"I get along all right. What were you talking to that old woman about?"

"She called me a gringo."

"You are a gringo."

"What's a gringo?"

"You who have conquered us."

"My people were conquered too."

"Who were your people?"

"We called ourselves the Confederacy."

"The gringo soldiers in gray! I know about the gringo soldiers in gray. They come here once, a long time ago. My father say they were just as bad as the gringo soldiers in blue."

Stone finished his burrito and washed it down with beer. "Paco, you know everybody in this town?"

"Sure do."

Stone took out the picture of Marie. "Ever see this woman?"

The boy stared at the picture. "She is very pretty, like a *princesa.* Who is she?"

"Friend of mine."

Paco pointed to the church across the bustling square. "You should go into that church over there and pray to the Blessed Mother that you find her. There was a big miracle here once, you hear about it?"

"The Virgin Mary appeared to a priest, right?"

"Yes, and the priest have the stigmata. His name was Padre Fernando, and he bleed from his hands and heart and feets, like *Jesús Cristo*. He is buried in the church, underneath the statue of the Blessed Mother. You go in there and pray that you find your *princesa*, and then you will find her, you will see. Come on. I take you."

Paco grabbed Stone's hand and dragged him across the square, passing guitar players, dancing girls, food vendors, and children chasing each other through the crowds. A flock of pigeons flew overhead to the top of the church steeple, where they perched and looked down into the square.

Stone and Paco approached the front of the church, which was illuminated by candles and torches. Throngs of people entered and departed through the wide-open doorway. Stone looked inside and hesitated; it seemed mysterious and strange.

Paco pushed him hard, and Stone found himself passing through the doorway, entering the church. It was mostly dark except for an altar in front, where a statue of the Virgin Mary stood in the light of candles, and people clustered around, praying on their knees.

Smaller altars were located along the walls of the church, where other people were praying, and as Stone's eyes adjusted to the darkness, he saw additional people praying on their knees in the pews. Someone played a guitar softly. Stone moved into the shadows and watched what was going on.

Stone believed vaguely in God, but never had seen anything quite like what was before him. People prayed fervently and deeply all across the church, and he couldn't help being moved by their devotion. They were true believers and their faith was strong, whereas he wasn't exactly sure of what he believed in.

Everyone's attention was centered around the statue of the Virgin at the front of the church placed on the spot where she'd appeared to Father Fernando. Stone wondered if he was witnessing pathetic superstition or a genuine miracle.

Before he knew what he was doing, he found himself moving with the rest of the pilgrims down the aisle toward the statue. He was caught up in the movement of bodies, and like a mighty wave it carried him toward the statue. As he drew closer, he could see that it was made of plaster, gaudily painted, chipped here and there, sort of a caricature of a pious woman with a halo, wearing a blue and white gown, looking up with doe eyes toward heaven and carrying an infant with a halo in her arms.

The statue looked cheap and mawkish to Stone, but it gave him an eerie feeling and his eyes were watering, probably from the incense and smoke from the candles. Standing to the side of the statue, he recalled what Paco had told him about praying for luck, so he closed his eyes and felt stupid as he asked: *Please send me somebody who's seen Marie.*

When he opened his eyes he saw a beautiful young Mexican woman with black hair and golden earrings approaching the statue down the middle of the aisle. She wore a white blouse and brown skirt, and dropped to her knees in front of the statue, crossing herself gracefully, clasping her hands together, and closing her eyes.

Her lips moved silently as she prayed, and Stone felt her religious zeal. She looked like a young madonna. *I wonder what she's praying for?*

The woman arose, adjusted her black shawl around her shoulders, and moved toward the door. Stone followed her, but some Mexicans walked in front of him, and by the time he pushed his way through them, she was gone.

He walked out of the church and looked around the square, but couldn't see her in the crowds of merrymakers. He stepped to the side and rolled himself a cigarette, lighting it with a match. He wasn't hungry anymore and felt like having a drink.

He saw an old cavalry sergeant walk by, his campaign hat askew on his head, his eyes glassy from too much booze. Stone walked up to him.

"Where can I get a drink around here?"

"La Rosita, down the street, but watch yer back."

Stone walked down the street, puffing his cigarette, hearing the strains of guitars, trumpets, and violins. Children laughed, and somebody shouted: *"Olé!"*

He passed a series of stores closed for the night, and halfway down the street came to a noisy adobe saloon with a sign that said LA ROSITA. It had two small windows that glowed red and two swinging doors. Stone hitched up his belt and walked toward the doors, pushing them open, and stepping into a dim smoky room with a bar on the left and tables on the right. The ceiling was low and somebody had nailed baskets to the walls for decoration. Mexicans, American soldiers, and American civilians drank and played cards raucously, and at the far end of the bar, the three Apache scouts Stone had seen with Lieutenant Lowell's cavalry column earlier in the day were huddled together drinking whiskey.

Stone walked toward the bar and placed his foot on the brass rail, his cigarette dangling out the corner of his mouth. The bartender, a Mexican with a bald head and a long flowing black mustache, sidestepped in front of him.

"Whiskey," Stone said.

The bartender placed a bottle and a glass in front of Stone, who poured himself a drink and drank it slowly. It was like swallowing flames.

La Rosita was a typical frontier bar except for the low ceiling and the presence of so many Mexicans. A small stage was against the far wall and Stone wondered what the entertainment was. Standing next to him was a lanky sergeant with his campaign hat on the back of his head, obviously quite drunk, with a curly red beard. He turned to Stone, stared for a few moments, and declared: "I'll be a son of a bitch!"

Stone looked at him, recognizing something familiar. "My God," he said.

The soldier drew himself to attention and saluted. "Sergeant Gerald McFeeley, First South Carolina Cavalry, reporting for duty, sir!"

Stone recognized McFeeley underneath his red beard and blue uniform. McFeeley had been one of his sergeants in old Troop C. They shook hands heartily, slapping each other on the shoulders.

"I can't believe my eyes," said McFeeley. "Is it really you, Cap'n?"

"It's me."

"You look like hell, if you don't mind me sayin' so."

"So do you. What're you doing out here?"

"Soldierin' is all I know, Cap'n. I took off one uniform and put on another, you might say." McFeeley threw back his shoulders and sang:

*"If you want to smell hell, boys,
join the cavalry—"*

Stone smiled as he listened to McFeeley howl the exuberant
driving rhythms of the old tune they'd sung around campfires
so long ago. It had been Jeb Stuart's favorite song, the unofficial anthem of Jeb Stuart's command.

McFeeley finished the song and held his glass of whiskey
in the air. "To old Troop C," he said.

Stone touched his glass to McFeeley's and together they
drank. It was like the old days, when they were fighting for
Bobby Lee, but now the two old soldiers were in a saloon on the
frontier, and the bitter taste of defeat was in their mouths.

"I guess you're disappointed in me," McFeeley said sadly.

"What makes you say that?"

"I'm wearin' the Yankee uniform now."

"It's not the Yankee uniform anymore. It's the uniform of
all Americans, no matter where they're from."

"I didn't know what to do with meself after the war, Cap'n,
so I joined the cavalry, but it ain't like the old days. These
Apaches are regular devils. They don't stand up and fight
you like men. They sneak up on you when you're not ex-
pectin' somethin', and slit yer throat before you know they're
there."

Stone looked down the bar at the three Apache scouts drinking at the end. "Some of them are on our side, I see."

"Don't ever trust any of 'em no matter whose side they're
on, and you'll live longer. What are you doin' out here?"

"Lookin' for somebody." Stone took the picture of Marie out
of his pocket and showed it to McFeeley. "Ever see her?"

"I remember this picture," McFeeley said. "You carried it
in the war, didn't you?"

"That's right."

"I ain't never seen the woman. You was goin' to marry her,
I recall. What happened to her?"

"That's what I'm trying to figure out."

McFeeley handed the picture back to Stone. "I hate to say
it, Cap'n, but you look kinda down on your luck."

"It's a hard life."

"Maybe you should join the cavalry. Twenty miles a day on beans and hay. It's better than nothin'."

"Maybe someday."

McFeeley's eyes took on a faraway look. "Do you ever think about Gettysburg?"

"All the time."

"Sometimes at night I dream about it. It's as if it happened just yesterday. You couldn't explain it to somebody. If they wasn't there, they'd never believe it."

Stone looked down into his glass and remembered July 3, 1863. The Hampton Brigade and Yankee cavalry under General George Armstrong Custer charged each other on the field of battle and collided with such force that horses turned end over end. Many cavalry soldiers on both sides had been crushed to death by fallen horses in the initial moments of combat, and then it was sabers and pistols at close range, a terrible bloody melee that lasted until dark, and when it was over neither side had won a clear-cut victory. Wade Hampton had been put out of action with a saber wound to the head, and Stone had been slashed several times and shot through the arm, but he still was able to lead old Troop C to Cress's Ridge where they took up positions for the night. It had been the worst day of his life.

"I don't think I could ever do it again," Stone said.

"Me neither, but we're still here, and the whiskey is better than ever." McFeeley raised his glass to his lips and guzzled down every last drop, then wiped his mouth with the back of his hand.

"Let me buy you a drink," Stone said.

"No, Cap'n—lemme buy you one. I'd consider it an honor."

McFeeley called the bartender and ordered the whiskey. Stone looked at McFeeley, thinking how strange life was. He'd never socialized with McFeeley during the war, because McFeeley had been an enlisted man and Stone an officer, and they'd never had an unofficial conversation, but now, four years later, they were like old friends.

The bartender poured the drinks, and this time they drank to Wade Hampton, who still was alive in South Carolina, active in politics according to the last news Stone had heard about him. Then they drank to Jeb Stuart, who'd been killed at Yellow Tavern on May 11, 1864, less than six miles from Richmond.

"I'll never forget old Jeb," McFeeley said, his eyes glittering with memories. "Do you remember how he used to wear his brown hat with the long black feather, troopin' the line?"

"I remember," Stone replied, looking across the interior of La Rosita, but seeing bearded Jeb Stuart in his fantastic uniform, atop his prancing horse.

"Crazy son of a bitch, wasn't he?"

"A little too crazy, maybe."

Jeb Stuart and Wade Hampton hadn't gotten along too well. Hampton thought Stuart was too erratic, a glory hound careless with the lives of his men. After Stuart was killed, Hampton took over his command. Under Stuart there had been frequent panics and much confusion, but everything settled down under Hampton, who'd been steady as a rock.

The two soldiers sipped their whiskey, lost in memories of war, and then McFeeley turned to Stone and looked up into his eyes. "What happened to us, Cap'n?" he asked plaintively.

"We lost a war—that's what happened to us."

"We were better men, Cap'n. You know we were."

"I used to think we were. Hell, I guess sometimes I still think we were, and other times I think maybe all of us on both sides were good men." Stone shrugged. "The Yankees had more of everything than we did, and that's why they beat us, but they didn't beat us because they were better men. Nobody was better than the old First South Carolina."

They stood at the bar silently for a few minutes, lost in reverie. Men shouted and shoved all around them, but it was as if Stone and McFeeley were in the eye of a hurricane, where all was peaceful and still.

Finally McFeeley raised his glass and drank it dry. "Well, Cap'n," he said, "I gotta git back to the post. They wake us up early in the mornin', you know what it's like." He held out his hand. "It was nice talkin' to you. How long you gonna be in town?"

"Don't know."

"Let's have a drink together before you hit the trail again."

"It's a deal."

They gripped each other's hands firmly, then McFeeley turned and made his way drunkenly toward the door.

Stone called the bartender and got another refill, which he

poured down his throat. McFeeley brought back the war. It seemed as if Gettysburg had been fought only last week.

Stone wondered if he'd ever get over the war. It kept coming back to him at odd moments when his mind was wandering or when something jogged his memory. He felt as if he'd lived a hundred lifetimes during those five years. He often dreamed about the great battles of the war, reliving every moment, every saber slash and every pistol shot. He thought it was a miracle that he'd survived, because so many of his friends had been killed, and indeed, virtually the entire top leadership of the Confederate Army had died on the field of battle, Stonewall Jackson, James Longstreet, and old Jeb Stuart among them.

He was amazed by things that he'd done during the war. The Yankees often used canisters in their cannons, and canisters were tin cans filled with balls of lead around an inch and a half in diameter. Canisters were fired directly into the Hampton Brigade at Gettysburg, tearing huge holes in the line, but Stone charged right into the thick of it, and every single man in old Troop C had followed him.

We must've been crazy, he thought, draining his glass. He called the bartender and got another refill, then gulped half of it down.

He was feeling light-headed from the whiskey, and didn't like remembering the war. Glancing around, he saw men guzzling whiskey. Stone had been drinking for most of his life, even when he was a teenager in South Carolina, but he'd never seen people drink the way they drank on the frontier. Nearly all the men drank virtually all the time. His own drinking had increased substantially since he came onto the frontier. It seemed to be the only thing to do.

He looked at the three Apache scouts at the end of the bar. Two of them pushed their empty glasses forward, spoke a few words with their comrade, and then turned around and walked out of the saloon, leaving the third Apache alone with his glass of whiskey.

The lone Apache was broad-shouldered and thick in the chest, with long straight black hair and a red bandanna tied around his head. He looked incongruous at the bar, a savage among American cowboys, card sharps, cavalry soldiers, and Mexicans.

Stone stared at him, fascinated and curious. He'd never spoken with an Apache before, and thought about going over and introducing himself. The worst thing that could happen was that the Apache would ignore him, but that wouldn't bother Stone. He'd been ignored before. Lots of people were wary of strangers.

The Apache appeared confused. His glass was empty, and he searched his pockets for money, the corners of his mouth turned down. Stone picked up his glass and walked down the bar toward the Apache.

The Apache heard him coming and spun around suddenly, measuring him with his eyes. The Apache wore a standard-issue blue cavalry shirt without insignia or rank, white pants, and a long white breechclout, with standard issue cavalry boots.

Stone stopped beside him and estimated his height at around five feet ten inches.

"Do you speak English?" Stone asked.

"Yes," the Apache replied gutturally.

"Can I buy you a drink?"

The Apache narrowed his eyes suspiciously. "Why you want to buy me a drink?"

"For the hell of it." Stone motioned to the bartender. "Two whiskeys."

The bartender poured the booze, and the Apache stared at the clear amber liquid trickling into his glass. Light from lanterns illuminated his face, and he appeared young, in his late twenties like Stone. When the bartender was finished, the Apache grasped the glass tightly and raised it to his lips, taking a gulp.

"What's your name?" Stone asked.

"Lobo."

"I'm John Stone."

Lobo looked at him. "I remember you. We find you on the desert today. You nearly become food for the vultures. Warriors were near you. If we did not come, they would have kill you. Did you see the vultures circling over your head? What you think they were there for? They were there for you."

Stone recalled the vultures circling over his head, but hadn't been aware they were waiting for him to be killed. "How do you know warriors were near me?"

Lobo snorted derisively. "I see them. They were on the hill

where we first see you. Three of them. They would have kill you. You are a fool."

"I'm new to this part of the country."

"You will not last long."

"You actually saw three warriors coming after me?"

Lobo nodded solemnly.

"Wasn't it your job to report anything you saw?"

"There was no danger."

"It was up to your commanding officer to make that decision."

Lobo turned down the corners of his mouth. "I have no commanding officer. I am not in your Army. I am not a bluecoat soldier."

"You're a scout, aren't you?"

"The bluecoat Army pays me to warn of danger. There was no danger."

Lobo raised the glass to his lips and took another gulp, and Stone could sense his strength and ferocity. There was a scar on Lobo's cheek and another on his left hand.

"I was standing down the bar there looking at you," Stone said, "and I was wondering about something."

"I saw you look at me. What do you want?"

"Why do you betray your people?"

Lobo's eyes clouded over for a moment, then he raised his chin an inch. "My business."

"Do you do it for the money?"

Lobo spat onto the floor. "That is what I think of money."

Stone took out his bag of tobacco and rolled himself a cigarette, then passed the tobacco to Lobo, who accepted it and rolled one for himself. Stone lit both cigarettes with a match. Lobo leaned one elbow on the bar and puffed his cigarette, closing one eye to keep the smoke out.

"You say you stand there at the bar looking at me," Lobo said. "Well, I stand here looking at you. I think to myself: *That white eyes is a warrior.* Is so?"

"I used to be a warrior, but not anymore."

"You were a bluecoat soldier?"

"I was a graycoat soldier."

"Ah. The graycoats. They lost."

"One side always has to lose."

"I think you are still a warrior, but you do not know anything about the desert. Do not ever go there alone again. My people will kill you. And you will not like the way they kill you. It will not be fun, I promise."

"Why don't you live with your people?"

"My business."

"If you don't do it for the money, what do you do it for?"

Lobo narrowed his eyes and said nothing.

"You must have a good reason," Stone said. "A warrior doesn't do anything unless he has a good reason."

Lobo raised his glass and drained it. "I go now," he said.

"What's your hurry?"

"You ask too many questions."

"I only asked you one question. I was a warrior too, as I told you, and I never would've betrayed my side for anything. You're obviously a man of honor, and I can't help wondering why you betray your side."

The bartender lifted Lobo's empty glass. "Care for another, gents?"

"Two more," Stone replied.

The bartender poured the drinks, and Lobo stood with his fists resting on the bar. His face was expressionless, but his body was rigid with tension. Then he turned to Stone and looked him in the eye.

"I hate Coyotero," he said.

"Who's Coyotero?"

"Coyotero has disgraced my sister, and I kill him someday."

"What about the other Apaches who work as scouts?"

"They do it for money and guns. They are fools, but they are good warriors. I tell you as one warrior to another: don't ever trust Apache."

"Can you be trusted?"

"No white eyes should ever trust Apache, because we hate you. You are killing us."

"I know we're crowding you off your land, but we want to live here too."

"We cannot live together. One of us has to die, and it will be the Apache."

"Why can't we live together in peace?"

Lobo laughed bitterly. "The only way you let us live in peace is if we move to reservation, where we live like rats. No, we are enemies until one of us is gone, and the one who is gone—that will be the Apache."

Stone couldn't help feeling sorry for him, because he understood how it felt to be part of a dying breed, like the Confederacy.

Stone heard the strum of guitars behind him. He turned around and saw that the stage had become lighted while he'd been talking with Lobo, and two Mexican guitarists were seated on chairs, playing a tune.

Then a young Mexican woman stepped onto the stage, and Stone recognized her as the pretty one he'd seen in the church praying so fervently before the plaster statue of Mary. She had flashing eyes and a broad smile, quite unlike the somber expression she'd worn in church.

She raised her hands and sang to the accompaniment of the guitarist. The song was sad, and her voice was clear and pure, strong enough to drown out the conversation and other extraneous noise in the saloon.

Stone gazed at her, stirred by a song he couldn't even understand, but she was pouring her soul into it, singing with the same passion that she'd brought to her prayer in the church.

Stone thought she was lovely, and he'd never seen anyone sing with such intensity. It was as though the song was important and she meant every word.

"Do you know what she's saying?" Stone asked Lobo.

"Something about love," Lobo replied, a note of boredom in his voice. "The Mexican girls—they always sing about love."

Stone returned his attention to the stage. He'd never been among Mexicans before, and it was all new to him. Americans usually hid their emotions, but the Mexican woman was cutting loose with everything she had.

Suddenly, in what seemed to be the middle of the song, the woman stopped singing, and the guitarists hit a final chord. The woman bowed, her long black hair dropping toward the floor, and everybody applauded loudly. Stone clapped his hands too, thinking of her kneeling before the altar in church.

She left the stage and was replaced by three Mexican women, who performed a dance to the accompaniment of the guitars. The woman who'd sung disappeared into the crowd.

"I am leaving," said Lobo.

"What's your hurry?" Stone replied. "I'll buy you another drink."

Lobo narrowed his eyes suspiciously. "Why you want buy me another drink?"

"I have a business proposition for you."

"A what?"

"A job."

"You want to pay me to work for you?"

"That's right. Let's have another drink, and then we'll talk about it."

Stone called for the bartender and ordered another round. Two cavalry soldiers argued loudly at the other end of the bar, and the Mexican dancers spun around on the stage, the hems of their dresses rising above their knees, their castanets clicking wildly, their eyes and teeth glittering, and the men close to the stage clapped their hands to the beat.

The bartender poured two more drinks for Stone and Lobo.

"I am getting drunk," Lobo said, raising the glass to his lips.

"So'm I."

"It is no good to get drunk."

"Why not?"

"It makes a warrior stupid."

"Then why do you do it?"

"Because it helps me see things."

"What kind of things."

"I don't trust you. You want something from me."

"That's right—I do want something from you, and I'll tell you what it is: I want you to take me to Tucson."

"How much?"

"Twenty dollars. I know you can get me there, because you are an Apache and the Apaches know the desert."

"Not interested."

"Why not?"

"Why should I take you to Tucson?"

"For twenty dollars."

"Money does not mean anything to me."

"Thirty dollars."

"Let me think about it."

Lobo drank some whiskey, his eyes half-closed. Stone remembered the Comanches he'd fought in Texas, and they hadn't looked much different from Lobo. It was strange to be standing at a bar talking with a wild Indian.

"It will be dangerous in the desert," Lobo said.

"It's dangerous everywhere—so what?"

"You really are a warrior."

"I just want to go to Tucson."

"A woman?"

"How did you know?"

"You are that kind of man."

"What kind of man are you?"

Lobo pulled his knife out of its sheath on his belt and held the blade with the sharp edge up. "This kind of man," he said.

Stone looked at the knife gleaming in the light of lamps and candles. "You're the man I want," Stone told him. "Take me to Tucson. I'll pay thirty dollars."

"It will be cheaper to take the stagecoach."

"The stagecoach might not get through."

Lobo grinned. "You are smarter than you look, white eyes."

"You could get through, Lobo. You're an Apache yourself. You know the desert."

"I will think about it."

"When will you tell me?"

"Maybe tomorrow."

"I don't have time to wait very long."

There was a commotion at the other end of the bar, and Stone turned around to look. The woman who'd sung was walking in his direction, and admirers applauded and whistled. Some of them offered to buy her a drink, but she shook her head and smiled, continuing to move toward Stone. Stone thought she was coming to speak with him, but when she came abreast of him she didn't look at him at all, and kept walking by, heading toward a door near the bar.

Lobo laughed. "You thought she was coming to see you. What a fool you are."

Her fragrance was like fresh flowers in the tobacco-laden air, and before Stone knew what he was doing, he was following her.

"Señorita," he said.

She ignored him, and he leapt in front of her, barring her way, looking down into her dark eyes.

"Señorita," he said, "you sing beautifully. I've never heard anything quite like it. Could I buy you a drink? Would you talk with me for a while?"

She had high cheekbones and lips like rose petals. "I saw you in church earlier, no?"

"Yes. I watched you praying. I wish I had your faith, señorita."

"You should never watch anyone pray. It is a personal thing."

"I couldn't help it. Your devotion was so deep."

"I am no saint, señor. You see what I do for a living."

"You sing about love. There's nothing wrong with that."

"There are many kinds of love. What is your name?"

"John Stone."

"I am Juanita Galindez. Yes, I will have a drink with you."

Stone led her to the spot at the bar beside Lobo, whose brow was wrinkled with worry.

"This is my friend Lobo."

"How do you do," Juanita said. "I have seen you here before. You work for the gringo soldiers, no?"

"Sometimes."

She turned to Stone. "I have never seen you before. When did you come to Santa Maria del Pueblo?"

"Today, shortly before I saw you in church."

"Why are you here?"

"I'm looking for a woman." Stone took out the photograph and showed it to her. "Ever see her?"

"No. Who is she?"

"Friend of mine."

Juanita smiled. "I think she is more than a friend."

"We were engaged to be married, and then I went away to war. When I returned, she was gone, and now I'm looking for her."

"I hope you find her someday. Is that what you were praying for in church?"

"That's right."

"I hope the Virgin answers your prayer."

"I hope she answers your prayer too. What were you asking for?"

"That is a secret."

Juanita ordered a glass of wine from the bartender, and when he brought it, she sipped daintily. Stone thought she had the face of a Spanish doll, but her body was womanly, with a full bosom and slim waist.

Lobo drained his glass and wiped his mouth with the back of his hand. "I go to the fort," he said to Stone. "I will see you here tomorrow night with my answer."

They shook hands, and Stone could feel raw power in the Apache's arm. Lobo turned and walked to the door.

Juanita leaned her back against the bar. "How did you two come to be friends?"

"We just started talking," Stone replied.

She shivered. "I am afraid of Apaches."

"Don't ever be afraid of anything. The worst thing that can happen to you is that you'll be killed, and everybody dies sooner or later."

"It is not death that I am afraid of. It is life. Sometimes life is very difficult."

"Tell me what's wrong, and maybe I can help you."

"No one can help me except God."

"Do you need money?" he asked.

"Not money."

"Then what?"

"I cannot say."

"If you can't say, how can I help you?"

"Why do you want to help me?"

"I don't know. What does it matter?"

She fluttered her long black lashes. "Too bad you belong to another woman, gringo."

"My name's John Stone."

"You are a crazy gringo."

"Why am I crazy?"

"You come into a place where you do not know anybody, and you start talking with an Apache. Don't you know anything about Apaches? They are killers. They even kill women and babies. Then you talk with me, and you do not know who I am. I might be somebody's woman, for all you know."

"Are you?"

"Yes."

"You're married?" he asked, surprised. "I didn't see a ring."

"I am not married, but I am somebody's woman."

"Do you love him?"

"What is love?"

"You were just singing a song about it, weren't you?"

"It was only a song."

"It sounded to me like it was much more than a song. It sounded like you meant it."

"It is my job to sound as if I meant it."

"I don't believe you were faking."

She shrugged. "Believe what you want. I knew I should not speak with you. I knew you would be trouble. You have trouble written all over your face."

"Why did you speak with me?"

She looked up at him. "I do not know. Maybe because you are like a wild horse. Do you know what the Apaches do with their horses? They ride them until they drop, and then they eat them."

"Apaches have a hard life."

"Everybody has a hard life."

"What's hard about your life?"

"There you go again."

"Why don't you come with me to Tucson?"

"You are going to Tucson?"

"That's right."

"With the Apache?"

"Maybe."

"He will kill you and eat your liver. If you go anywhere with an Apache, you are crazier than I thought. You should never trust an Apache."

"He told me the same thing."

"But you trust him anyway?"

"Yes, I do."

"How can you trust a man who tells you not to trust him?"

"We understand each other."

She shook her head sadly. "You are going to be one dead gringo pretty soon, I think so. The bones of many men like you are on the desert, picked clean by the vultures and the rats."

Juanita sipped her wine, and Stone studied her proud Spanish profile. She turned toward the front door of La Rosita.

"I must go," she said. "Excuse me."

"What's wrong?"

"Stay away from me."

She placed her half-empty glass on the bar and turned in the direction of the back door where she'd been headed when Stone first spoke with her. Suddenly, out of the crowd, a husky Mexican man appeared with rows of silver disks affixed to the outer seams of his pants. Grabbing Juanita roughly by the shoulder, he spun her around. He had a black mustache and curly black hair, and was in his mid-thirties.

"What are you doing with that gringo!" he hollered.

She looked frightened. "It was nothing. Only business."

The Mexican turned to Stone, glowering, and Stone glowered back.

"Who in hell are you?" the Mexican asked.

"Just another gringo," Stone replied.

"I think you had better get out of here *rápido* if you know what is good for you."

"I'm not ready to leave yet."

Juanita looked at Stone and pleaded: "Please do as he says, señor. It is best for everybody."

Stone stood with his legs spread apart, looking at the Mexican. "Who's he?"

"I am his woman."

The Mexican stared back at Stone. "You have made a big mistake, gringo. You should have left while I gave you the chance."

Stone stood solidly, studying the Mexican, waiting to see what he'd do. He didn't go through five years of war to get pushed around by a Mexican in a frontier saloon. Drinkers and gamblers stepped back out of the way. The bartender ducked behind the bar. Everything became still.

The Mexican man reached to his belt and pulled out a knife with a six-inch blade. He held the knife in his right hand with the blade up.

Juanita moved toward the Mexican. "Leave him alone, Rodrigo. He is only a drunken gringo. He is not worth the trouble."

"Get away from me!"

"Please, Rodrigo!"

Rodrigo pushed her out of his way, then stepped toward Stone. "I am going to kill you," he said.

Stone reached into his boot and pulled out his Bowie knife; it had an eight-inch blade. "Not today."

Both men moved into the knife fighter's crouch, their blades before them, light glinting on the steel.

Rodrigo was shorter than Stone, but with more weight. His midsection was covered by a thick black leather belt with an ornately carved silver buckle. Stone's cavalry hat was slanted low over his eyes.

They moved closer and began to circle. Stone concentrated on Rodrigo's knife, waiting to see where it would go.

Rodrigo beckoned with his free hand and smiled. "Come closer," he said. "What are you afraid of?"

Stone moved his left foot forward suddenly, then drew it back, feinting a charge, but Rodrigo didn't fall for it.

"You will have to do better than that, my friend," Rodrigo said.

Rodrigo bent his knees and got even lower. He moved his blade back and forth as if threshing grain. This forced Stone to get lower too, so he could reach the soft parts of Rodrigo's body.

They continued to circle each other. Rodrigo tossed his knife from one hand to another, but Stone remained steady and poised. One wrong move and he was dead.

Stone glimpsed Juanita behind Rodrigo's shoulder in the crowd. Her face was pale as she hugged her waist.

Suddenly Rodrigo lunged forward with his knife, and Stone darted adroitly out of the way, taking a swipe at Rodrigo's arm, slicing off a piece of flesh.

Blood oozed out of the wound on Rodrigo's arm, soaking into the billowy sleeve of his white shirt. His eyes narrowed and the corners of his mouth turned down. He stamped his foot twice, feinting another charge, but Stone wasn't fooled. Stone changed direction suddenly and circled Rodrigo the other way.

Rodrigo followed Stone carefully with his eyes. A drop of blood fell from Rodrigo's arm to the floor, and the wound hurt. Stone had drawn first blood.

Rodrigo shouted, darting his foot forward and feinting another charge, but again Stone didn't fall for it. Then Rodrigo charged again, and this time it was no feint. Stone took another swing at Rodrigo's arm, and Rodrigo grabbed his wrist, while thrusting the point of his knife toward Stone's belly.

Stone's free hand clamped onto Rodrigo's wrist, and both men held on to each other tightly. Their faces were so close Stone could smell the chili and onions on Rodrigo's breath. They pressed their knives forward with one arm, and held their opponent's knives away with their other arm.

They strained against each other, and neither made any progress. Stone saw beads of perspiration drip down Rodrigo's forehead, and the crowd was howling for blood.

Rodrigo stepped back and to the side, let go of Stone's knife arm, and twisted his own knife arm free from Stone's grasp. Stone suddenly found himself pushing against thin air, and he went flying forward into the crowd. They got out of the way and he crashed into a table, rolling onto his back and kicking wildly.

His boot caught Rodrigo in the stomach as Rodrigo was coming in for the kill, and Rodrigo went sprawling backward toward the bar. Stone jumped to his feet and rushed after him. Rodrigo bounced off the bar and leapt at Stone, slashing at his face. Stone grabbed Rodrigo's wrist and stabbed his own knife toward Rodrigo's big belly.

Rodrigo grunted as he wrapped his fingers around Stone's arm, and both men were locked together closely again. Rodrigo swore in Spanish, heaving against Stone, but Stone was steady as a mountain and didn't budge. Meanwhile, Stone was unable to push Rodrigo back.

The crowd hollered. Rodrigo snaked his foot behind Stone and tripped him. Stone lost his balance and fell to the floor, still holding Rodrigo's wrist. The two men rolled across the wooden planks, knocking over a spittoon, each trying to achieve the advantage that would permit him to rip his opponent.

They came to a stop against the bar. Stone was on the bottom and Rodrigo on top.

"You are a dead gringo," Rodrigo said between clenched teeth as he pushed the point of his knife toward Stone's throat.

Stone found himself straining against Rodrigo's strength and weight. He looked up and saw the tip of Rodrigo's knife dropping inch by inch toward his throat, and if Stone didn't do something quickly, he'd be impaled on the end of it.

Stone took a deep breath and drew together all his strength, then heaved and bucked wildly. Rodrigo lost his balance, and both men went rolling across the floor again, gnashing their teeth, trying to stab each other.

They crashed against a table and came to a stop, but this time Stone was on top with his knife pointed down at Rodrigo's face. Stone leaned on his knife, which moved inexorably toward Rodrigo's cheek. Rodrigo's eyes bulged out of his head and he bared his teeth like a wild animal as he strained against Stone, trying to hold him back.

Then suddenly Rodrigo made a wild desperate dodging motion, and the point of Stone's knife jabbed down into the floorboards. Rodrigo jumped to his feet with a cry of triumph and slashed wildly at Stone, cutting open his shoulder. Stone yanked his blade out of the floorboards and leapt up, facing Rodrigo.

"Got you that time, gringo," Rodrigo said.

The two combatants circled each other again, and Lobo was in the crowd watching every movement. He'd been outside, walking toward his horse, when he heard the uproar in the saloon, and rushed back to see what was going on. Something told him the crazy white warrior had gotten himself in trouble, and when he entered the saloon, that's what he saw.

Lobo watched the knife fight intently, not missing a nuance. The combatants seemed evenly matched. Stone was stronger, but the Mexican appeared to have greater skill in knife fighting.

Lobo had been in many knife fights and knew that basically it was psychological. You had to outmaneuver your opponent or trick him in some way, get him off balance and force him to open himself up to your blade.

Both men were trying to do that, but neither was having any success. Fatigue would begin to play a part soon. Someone would get careless, and his opponent would take advantage.

Lobo watched the two men circle each other in the middle of the crowd. John Stone was fast and strong like a mountain lion, whereas the Mexican reminded Lobo of a bear, heavy and extremely dangerous. It was an interesting combination, and Lobo hoped Stone would win. He didn't know why he wanted Stone to win, because he had no great love for white eyes, but there was something about Stone that he admired.

Stone looked at Rodrigo and felt frustrated. Somehow he couldn't break through the Mexican's guard. The Mexican was a skilled knife fighter, whereas Stone was best with fists, pistols, and rifles. *Somehow I'll have to get him to make a mistake*, Stone thought.

Stone changed direction, dodged, changed direction again, feinted a charge, and then stepped back to see if he'd moved Rodrigo out of position.

Rodrigo laughed at him. "You are a dumb gringo. I think I kill you right now."

Rodrigo took a swipe at Stone's belly, and Stone jumped backward to avoid the tip of Rodrigo's knife. Rodrigo leapt forward and slashed at Stone again, and this time Stone couldn't get out of the way in time. The point of Rodrigo's knife ripped across the front of Stone's shirt, drawing a thin red line.

It hurt but Stone gritted his teeth and held steady. The thin red line became thicker as blood oozed out onto the torn shirt. It was a superficial flesh wound but it bled freely and sooner or later a man could become weak from loss of blood. That added a new element to the knife fight. Stone couldn't wait any longer for Rodrigo to make a mistake. He had to carry the fight to Rodrigo and defeat him quickly.

Rodrigo grinned fiendishly. "How did that feel, gringo?"

Stone ignored the pain and got low, looking for an opening, but there was nothing. Once in a knife fight he'd nearly cut off his opponent's knife arm; should he try that now? Or should he go for Rodrigo's throat, the quick kill?

Stone rushed toward Rodrigo, tossed his knife from his right hand to his left hand, and then, as Rodrigo turned to face the threat from a new direction, Stone flipped the knife back to his right hand, but Rodrigo was ready for the trick and whacked Stone's knife upward with his own knife. Stone's knife flew into the air and over the heads of the people in the crowd.

"Now I have got you where I want you, gringo," Rodrigo said.

Both men faced each other in the middle of the circle, and Stone had no knife. He realized now that he'd made a mistake when he'd tried to get fancy, but it was too late to do anything about it now.

Rodrigo laughed as he feinted with his knife, and Stone jumped out of the way. Rodrigo feinted again, and Stone dodged once more.

"What is the matter with you, gringo?" Rodrigo asked playfully. "Do you have ants in your pants?"

Rodrigo advanced toward Stone, and Stone stepped backward, holding both his fists up, blood spreading down the front of his shirt.

"I am going to skin you alive," Rodrigo said to Stone. "I am going to cut off your nose and your ears."

Rodrigo feinted once, then charged. Stone dived on his knife arm, grabbed it tightly, spun around, and threw Rodrigo over his shoulder. Rodrigo crashed into the wall and Stone pounced on him, punching him in the mouth, pulping his lips, but Rodrigo swung wildly with his knife, and that made Stone step back.

Rodrigo got to his feet and wiped the blood off his mouth. "Not a bad move, gringo," he said. "It was your last one, I think."

Stone waited for him in the middle of the floor. He'd have to get past Rodrigo's knife somehow and knock him out.

Something flashed in front of Stone, and he looked down to see his Bowie knife land at his feet. Someone had thrown it to him, and without a moment's hesitation, he bent over and snatched it up.

Rodrigo's face clouded with anger when he saw that Stone was armed again. "Who is the filthy bastard who did that?" he shouted.

Lobo the Apache stepped through the crowd. "Me."

"I will kill you next, Indian."

"You will kill nobody at all tonight," Lobo replied.

Rodrigo snarled like a wild beast and charged Stone, pushing the point of his knife toward Stone's belly, and Stone dodged out of the way like a matador. Rodrigo stopped in his tracks and turned around.

"You are afraid of the blade, eh, gringo? Well if I were you, I would be afraid of it too, because it will drink your blood soon."

Stone took a deep breath. He'd have to anticipate Rodrigo's thrusts, and counter before Rodrigo could get set again.

Rodrigo tossed his knife between his hands, a confident smile on his face. He had a reputation as a fierce fighter. The crowd expected him to win.

Meanwhile, the few Americans in the saloon urged Stone on. The circle tightened around Stone and Rodrigo. Juanita felt herself being moved forward. She was sure Rodrigo would beat her worse than ever after he killed John Stone.

Rodrigo darted to the left, darted to the right, and charged Stone, who timed him coming in and kicked him in the chops. Rodrigo saw stars for a moment, and when he regained consciousness he was stumbling backward, dropping to his back on the floor.

Stone jumped on him and jabbed his knife with all his strength toward Rodrigo's throat, but Rodrigo spun out at the last moment and Stone's knife stuck into the floorboards. Rodrigo, on his knees, lashed out at Stone and ripped a six-inch gash along his ribs, while Stone, also on his knees, yanked his knife out of the floorboards and swung at Rodrigo's face, but Rodrigo leaned back and Stone's knife whistled harmlessly through the air.

Stone and Rodrigo jumped to their feet, and Rodrigo looked at the blood dripping out of Stone's side.

"Got you again, eh, gringo? How does it feel to bleed like a pig?"

Stone felt pain all across his upper body. Somehow he had to settle down and kill Rodrigo.

Someone moved between him and Rodrigo, and it was Juanita, her arms held stiffly down her sides and her hands balled into fists. She faced Rodrigo and said: "Please do not kill him! Do it for me, Rodrigo!"

"Get out of my way," Rodrigo replied in an ugly voice from deep in his throat. "I will take care of you later."

"He is innocent, and it will be a sin."

"Innocent?" Rodrigo asked. "No one is innocent, especially not this gringo."

Juanita turned and looked at Stone. "Tell him you are sorry, señor. Get down on your knees and beg him for your life. That is your only chance, because he is going to kill you."

"Do as he says," Stone said to her. "Get out of the way before you get hurt."

"This is my fault," Juanita said. "I should never have spoken with you, gringo. Your death will be a stain on my soul forever."

"Move," Stone told her softly.

She stepped back into the crowd, and near her Stone saw Lobo the Apache.

"Go for his belly," Lobo said. "Remember who you are."

Stone spread his legs and went into his crouch again, holding his knife steady before him as blood dripped down from his shirt onto his jeans.

"Are you ready to die, gringo?" Rodrigo asked.

Stone said nothing, but his eyes were fastened on Rodrigo, looking for an opening or a sign of weakness, ready to make the most of any opportunity.

Rodrigo screamed viciously and rushed toward Stone, punching his knife toward Stone's belly, and Stone stepped to his left, wielding his knife like his old cavalry saber, slashing Rodrigo's right bicep almost to the bone. Rodrigo howled and spun around, facing Stone, trying to raise his knife, but the deep tendons in his arm were severed and his knife wouldn't come up. Stone backswung with his knife and caught Rodrigo on the throat, nearly cutting his head off. Blood gushed out as if from a hose, and Rodrigo's face suddenly blanched. Rodrigo's head leaned to the side at a crazy angle, attached to his body only by his spinal cord and a few sinews of flesh. Rodrigo stared at Stone in disbelief, and Stone rammed his blade to the hilt into Rodrigo's stomach.

The crowd screamed. Blood welled out of Rodrigo's mouth, and he swayed from side to side. He looked at Stone and took two drunken tottering steps toward him, then his eyes rolled up into his head and he collapsed onto the floor, where he lay still in a widening pool of blood.

There was silence in the saloon as everyone stared at Rodrigo's corpse. Three Mexican men stepped out of the crowd and dropped to their knees around Rodrigo, rolling him onto his back. Rodrigo looked grotesque with his head nearly detached from his body and his clothes drenched with blood. Stone took a step backward, wiped his knife on his pant leg, and dropped it into his boot.

Juanita moved toward him. "You must leave this town at once! Rodrigo's men will kill you! They are *bandidos*!"

"What about you?" he asked. "What will Rodrigo's men do to you?"

"Do not worry about me! Go quickly!"

A group of Mexicans advanced toward Stone from the other side of the saloon, and their faces showed bad intentions. An expression of terror came over Juanita's face, and Stone turned to face them.

There were five of them, and they approached from the front and sides, their hands reaching for their guns. Stone dodged to the left, whipped out his Colts, and triggered as fast as he could.

The saloon filled with gunsmoke and the roar of gunfire. There was a tremendous boom that shook the coal-oil lamps. Stone felt something rip into his shoulder, but stood his ground and kept firing. Men shrieked and lurched in the smoke in front of him, a bullet whizzed past his ear so closely he could feel its heat, but he continued to whack those triggers.

There was another boom, and it made Stone's ears ring. Stone pulled his triggers and held his Colts level, and he was in the war again, riding into the teeth of the enemy at the head of old Troop C.

No one stood in front of him anymore. He relaxed the fingers on his triggers. The saloon became silent, and he could smell the acrid gunsmoke.

Five bullet-riddled bodies lay sprawled all over the floor in front of him. *Did I get them all?*

Lobo, carrying a shotgun, moved toward him from the left. "We best get out of here."

Lobo's face floated in front of Stone, then began to fade. Stone became dizzy and staggered a few steps. A wave of ferocious pain burst out of his left shoulder and passed like a wave over his body. He staggered a few steps more, trying to stay on his feet, he had to get moving because he knew he was in danger.

Only his will kept him up. He saw Juanita running toward

him out of the fog and heard her scream. She reached for him, and then everything went black.

Stone's knees gave out and he went crashing to the floor.

In a large cave at the base of the Canutillo Mountains, Antonio Vargas slept on a large bed, his arms around Teresa Gonzalez, and both of them were naked.

The bed was in a corner of the cave, hidden by a curtain. Beds and a table and chairs were scattered on the other side of the curtain in the main part of the cave. It was night, and a bird cried far out on the desert.

Antonio was nineteen years old, with the crude tattoo of a cross on his left shoulder. Dark-skinned, a thin mustache covering his upper lip, he snuggled closer to Teresa, nuzzling his cheek against her breast.

She had long wavy black hair and was full-bodied, with dark thick eyebrows.

In the depths of his slumber, Antonio sensed somebody near him. In a flash he was awake, reaching under his pillow for his pistol.

"It is me, Antonio," said a voice above him.

Antonio looked up and saw Miguel, and behind him were other members of the band, including some of the women.

"What happened?" asked Antonio.

"A terrible thing," Miguel said. "Rodrigo has been killed."

Antonio sat bolt upright in bed, suddenly wide awake. "What do you mean?"

"He got in a fight and was killed."

Antonio took a deep breath. "You are sure of this?"

"I saw it with my own eyes, and so did the others."

Antonio looked at them, and they stood silently before him as if in church. Antonio felt as if he were dreaming.

"Where is he now?" Antonio asked, and his voice sounded as if someone else were talking.

"On the porch."

"Get out of here and let me put my pants on."

They left his small enclosed area, and he and Teresa got out of bed. She dropped her shift over her head, and he pulled on his pants. They came out from behind the curtain and were led out of the cave and into the moonlight.

A vast landscape of buttes and spires stretched before him, glowing faintly. Stars blazed across the sky and the moon was a huge effulgent globe. Lying on the rock shelf in front of the cave was the body of Rodrigo, covered with blood and gore. Bodies of the other five dead bandits were sprawled nearby.

Antonio gazed down at Rodrigo, and tears filled his eyes.

"Who did this thing?" he asked.

"A stranger," said Miguel.

"Why did you let him get away?"

"We were not with him. We were in another cantina." Miguel explained how they split up after they arrived in town. Rodrigo and some of them went to La Rosita, and Miguel, with the rest, stopped by La Paloma. Later some of the women who'd gone with Rodrigo ran back with news of the fight.

"Who saw the fight?" Antonio asked.

Clara stepped forward, another full-bodied woman, around thirty years old. "It was over Juanita," she said. "Juanita was flirting with the stranger, and Rodrigo catch them together."

"What was this stranger's name?"

Miguel cleared his throat, and nervously turned the brim of the hat in his hands. "We ask around, but nobody know. He was a stranger like I said."

Antonio looked at Clara. "What did he look like?"

"He was a big hombre, like this." Clara held her hand in the air, and Antonio realized the stranger was taller than he. "He was very big this way too." She held out her hands to show the size of Stone's wide shoulders. "His hair was light. He kill Rodrigo, and an Indian help him kill the other men. The Indian, he have a shotgun. His name is Lobo and he worked for the Army. He took the stranger with him and they ran away. Nobody knows where they went."

"Where is Juanita?"

"She went with them."

Antonio knelt on one knee beside Rodrigo's stiffening corpse. It was unbelievable to think that someone had killed Rodrigo with a knife. Rodrigo had been a great fighter and had killed many men, but now he himself had been killed. The stranger who killed him must have been an even greater fighter, and that was hard to imagine.

Tenderly Antonio touched his hand to Rodrigo's head, and

it moved away from Rodrigo's body. Antonio's eyes widened with horror when he realized that Rodrigo's head had nearly been cut off!

Antonio withdrew his hand quickly. He stood, clenched his teeth. "Saddle up the horses," he said. "We're going after them."

3

THE BUGLER BLEW reveille as dawn broke on Fort Kimball. Lieutenant Lowell opened his eyes and groaned. Samantha, his wife, stirred beside him.

"Stay in bed with me," she murmured. "Tell them you're sick."

"I have an appointment with the colonel at nine."

"Who's more important to you, the colonel or me?"

"The colonel."

Lieutenant Lowell rolled out of bed and lit a thin cigar from the private stock his father sent him regularly from Boston. Then he stood and pulled on his pants. He walked to the window, separating the drapes.

The horizon in the east was orange and red, and before him lay the parade ground, a few scattered soldiers running across it. On the other side of the parade ground were more adobe buildings similar to the one Lieutenant Lowell and Samantha lived in. Enlisted men were billeted at the north end of the fort, with married personnel to the south.

Samantha washed her face in the basin. "Every day I hate this place more. Even when I sleep at night, I get that damned alkali on me."

"It's your imagination," he said, puffing his cigar, thrusting his arms through the sleeves of his shirt. "There's no alkali in here."

"Yes, there is. I can feel it. It's everywhere, and it's driving me crazy."

She walked to the kitchen to light the stove for breakfast. Lieutenant Lowell sat on the bed and pulled on his cavalry boots, thinking about his meeting with Colonel Braddock. He had to present the report on his patrol, and Colonel Braddock always asked difficult questions that Lieutenant Lowell tried to anticipate in advance.

Standing, he strapped on his saber. Most officers on the frontier didn't wear them, but Lieutenant Lowell considered his saber the ultimate symbol of the cavalry. He'd been a member of the West Point Fencing Team.

Samantha dropped something in the kitchen. "Damn!" she said. "Son of a bitch!"

Lieutenant Lowell walked into the kitchen. "You swear worse than my troopers. I wish you'd cut it out. Somebody's liable to hear you."

"I don't care if they do hear me," she said. "I want the whole world to hear me. I hate this place. I want to get out of here. I know we've been over this a million times, but I'm sorry, I don't see why you don't ask your uncle to get us a transfer back east."

"First of all, please lower your voice, because they probably can hear you all the way to Santa Maria del Pueblo. Second, I've told you numerous times that I don't want any special favors from my uncle."

He came up behind her and hugged her, cupping her breasts in his hands. She closed her eyes and placed her hands on his arms. "I love you, Josh, but you're never home and I'm here all alone most of the time in this terrible place."

"It's not Beacon Hill, but I thought you'd get used to it."

"I'm not getting used to it. I hate it. Do you understand what I'm saying? I'm losing my mind."

"The other officers' wives find things to do."

"I never met a duller group of women in my life. Most of them have never heard a concert or seen a play. Most of them don't even read. All they can talk about is their children."

There was a knock at the door, and Samantha turned around in Lieutenant Lowell's arms. "Who's that?"

Lieutenant Lowell released her and walked toward the door. He opened it and saw a sergeant with a red beard standing in front of him. The sergeant wasn't in his troop, but Lieutenant Lowell had seen him around the fort and had formed an overall good impression of him.

The sergeant stood at attention and saluted smartly. "Sergeant Gerald McFeeley reporting, sir. I hate to bother you so early in the morning, sir, but there's something important that I have to talk with you about."

Lieutenant Lowell was mystified. What could a sergeant from another troop possibly have to talk with him about?

"What is it?"

"It's about Cap'n Stone, sir."

"Who?"

"The gennelman you met up with yesterday when you was on patrol, sir. I understand you and he became friendly, is that right, sir?"

"What's on your mind, Sergeant?"

"Cap'n Stone is in trouble, sir. I heard from some of my men that he killed a Mexican outlaw named Rodrigo Vargas last night in La Rosita, and the Mexican's friends are after Cap'n Stone to kill him. Cap'n Stone was wounded bad, and I was wonderin' if there was some way you could help."

Lieutenant Lowell remembered Stone. "What do you want me to do?"

"Take a patrol out and look for him. Maybe you can get to him before the Mexicans, because you know what they'll do if they find him."

"We don't have any jurisdiction over civilians, as I'm sure you know."

"Cap'n Stone was my commanding officer during the war, and a finer soldier there never was. Do you think you could do somethin', sir?"

"I'd have to speak with Colonel Braddock."

"Would you try?"

Lieutenant Lowell puffed his cigar as he looked at the tall lanky sergeant standing in front of him. He recalled meeting Stone yesterday and had liked him instantly. Stone had seemed a little jaded by his experiences in the war, but that was under-standable. He'd gone to West Point.

"Of course I'll speak with the colonel," Lieutenant Lowell told Sergeant McFeeley. "I'll see him this morning and bring it up."

A smile came over Sergeant McFeeley's face. "Thank you, sir. I appreciate it. One more thing, sir. If you take out a patrol, do you think I could go along."

"I'll see what I can do, but tell me something, Sergeant. If Stone was wounded so badly, how did he get away?"

"One of the Apache scouts helped him, sir. He had a Mexican woman with him too, my men told me."

Lieutenant Lowell returned to the kitchen, where Samantha was placing two platters of eggs and sausages on the table. "What was that all about?"

"The fellow I told you about yesterday, the former Confederate officer, evidently killed a Mexican last night at one of the cantinas in town."

"Is that the one you said you were going to invite to dinner?"

"Yes."

"And he killed somebody? I thought you said he was nice."

"He was."

"Doesn't sound so nice to me."

"Those cantinas aren't exactly tea parties."

"What kind of man would go to a place like that?"

"There's nothing else to do in Santa Maria del Pueblo."

She pointed her finger at him. "That's exactly what I keep telling you. There's nothing to do here. Why can't we go back east, Josh? What is it that you like so much here?"

"It's hard to explain." He sat at the table and picked up a knife and fork. "There's something about the place. It's a beautiful land."

"I thought it was beautiful too when I first got here," she said, sitting opposite him, "but it became tiresome awfully quick. Maybe one of these days I'll go to a cantina and kill a Mexican."

"Don't make a joke out of it, Samantha. The man's life is in danger."

"I'm the one you're married to, remember?"

"I remember, but I have certain duties and obligations."

"What about your duties and obligations to me?"

"I do everything for you that I can. You knew I wanted to become a soldier when we were married. It's not as if it's a big surprise."

"I never realized it'd be like this."

"I think you ought to stop complaining and start making the best of what we've got here. It's not so bad."

"Maybe it's not so bad for you, because you're out riding horses with your men all the time, playing soldier boy while I'm stuck here with nothing to do. You're having fun, but *I'm not*."

He decided to stop arguing with her. It never led anywhere, and he had an appointment with Colonel Braddock that required his attention. "We'll talk about this later," he said.

"One of these days you'll come home from a patrol, and I won't be here," she replied. "Then maybe you'll wake up."

It wasn't the first time she had threatened to leave. She did it all the time, and he was used to it. She continued to harangue him as he ate quickly, thinking about the report he had to deliver to Colonel Braddock.

She banged her fist on the table. "You're ignoring me."

He covered his ears with his hands. "Please stop talking so loud."

"I hate it when you ignore me."

"I told you we'll talk about it later. I have an important report to make."

"Everything is important except me! You have plenty of time for anybody else, but not your wife! You'll do anything for those stupid drunken soldiers of yours, but you don't do anything for me!"

Lieutenant Lowell recalled overhearing the men talking in the barracks once. Sergeant Flynn had told the younger troopers: "The only thing to do if you're havin' an argument with a woman is grab your hat and run."

He arose from the table, wiped his mouth with his napkin, and walked toward the bedroom.

"Where are you going?" Samantha screamed.

"To work," he called out as he placed his campaign hat on his head. Picking up his leather portfolio, he headed for the front door.

"Come back here!"

But Lieutenant Lowell was already on the porch, jumping to the ground, on his way to Colonel Braddock's command post on the other side of Fort Kimball. Samantha watched him go, a scowl on her pretty face.

Lieutenant Lowell walked briskly across the parade ground, glad to be away from her, because her nagging was driving him crazy. She'd been wonderful back in Boston, but became a harpy after a few weeks at Fort Kimball.

Lieutenant Lowell didn't know what to do with her, but didn't have time to think about it. He had to prepare for his meeting with the colonel, and he knew he wouldn't be at his best because Samantha had flustered him. She didn't understand how she was undermining his career by behaving as she did. A woman should support a man in his career, not continually cut him down.

He tried to push her out of his mind. Around him, soldiers marched about, sergeants calling the cadence. The sun rose in the sky and Lieutenant Lowell could feel its warmth; it was going to be a hot day. He pulled out his gold watch, a gift from his father, and had forty-five minutes before his meeting with the colonel.

A trooper walking toward him saluted, and Lieutenant Lowell saluted back. Already he was feeling better. There was something about military life he loved. He didn't want to spend his life sitting behind a desk, making money like his father, when he could be in the great outdoors, serving his country.

Samantha didn't know how he felt. All she wanted was to attend plays and concerts with her friends, and talk about the latest poets and artists.

The officers' club was a complex of adobe structures attached to the BOQ (Bachelor Officers' Quarters). Lieutenant Lowell went inside and handed his hat to the orderly in the white jacket.

"Bring me a cup of coffee in the library, will you?" Lieutenant Lowell said.

To the left was the Officers' Mess, where the unmarried

officers were having breakfast. Lieutenant Lowell proceeded down the hallway to the library, a small room with a few bookcases and some chairs. He sat near the window, opened his portfolio, took out his report. The orderly arrived a few minutes later with the coffee.

Lieutenant Lowell sipped the coffee and looked at his handwritten pages, but his ears still rang with the sound of Samantha's voice. He could hear her criticizing and cajoling him, and there was no escape. Fort Kimball was a small post. He was either on duty with his men or home with her. He needed to go someplace to rest, but there was no place.

Sometimes he thought about sending her back east and getting a divorce, but he loved her and didn't want to be without a woman. Bachelor officers on the frontier became drunk and dissolute fairly rapidly, from what he'd observed so far. Some became involved with loose women in town, which was harmful to their careers. Lieutenant Lowell had observed that officers who'd graduated from West Point and had solid marriages were the ones who achieved high rank, while the others languished in the lower commissioned ranks until they either retired or were cashiered for drunkenness or some other dereliction or malfeasance.

Lieutenant Lowell loved the Army. It was a healthy decent life, and he was serving his country. He loved the camaraderie of the barracks and admired old war dogs like Colonel Braddock and Sergeant Flynn.

Samantha was spoiling it all for him with her constant tirades, and when she was among the other officers and wives, she spoke disparagingly of the Army. He realized now that Samantha was something of a snob, and maybe he shouldn't've married her, but she was beautiful and vivacious, and he loved to hold her in his arms. She made him feel alive and special, and he couldn't wait to get her in bed at night, where she was a wildcat.

He was in love with her and in love with the Army at the same time, but they were like oil and water; they didn't mix. His handwriting on the pages before him blurred, and he realized he was thinking about Samantha again instead of preparing for his report.

He sipped coffee and forced himself to concentrate, but soon found himself thinking about John Stone, who was wounded, on the desert running for his life from Mexican outlaws. Stone had the aura of command about him yesterday, although he'd been dusty and sweaty, wandering through Apache-infested territory like a tenderfoot. It was interesting how former officers like John Stone inspired a lifelong loyalty in enlisted men like Sergeant McFeeley. That surely was the mark of a superior officer, the kind of leader Lieutenant Lowell wanted to become.

Once again, he realized his mind was wandering. Gritting his teeth, he forced himself to focus on his report. *I've got to be letter-perfect this time,* he said to himself. *I don't want to make any more mistakes in front of Colonel Braddock.*

Colonel Braddock sat behind his desk, smoking a cigar. He was sixty years old, had white hair thinned out on top, and a swooping white mustache stained with nicotine. Behind him was a window overlooking the parade ground, and to the left of that, hanging from the wall, was a photograph of Ulysses S. Grant, the President of the United States and his former commander during the Civil War.

Colonel Braddock read a report that Captain Poole, his intelligence officer, had just delivered to him. It said Apaches were marauding worse than ever throughout the area, burning farm buildings, massacring settlers, stealing horses and cattle, and, in general, terrorizing everyone. Local politicians were clamoring for the Army to do something, but Colonel Braddock didn't know what to do.

The Apaches played hit and run. They ranged over a wide territory, and disappeared into the desert when they finished their bloody depredations. It was difficult to track them down, even with Apache scouts, and sometimes Colonel Braddock questioned the loyalty of the scouts themselves. For all he knew, they might be spies. Frequently they deserted the Army after receiving new rifles and ammunition. They were unpredictable, unreliable, and unfathomable.

The principal tribe in the area was headed by old Jacinto, said to be in his sixties now, but still an implacable foe of the white settlers. Colonel Braddock wanted to speak with Jacinto and make a treaty with him, but so far Jacinto had scorned all the overtures that Colonel Braddock had advanced.

All Colonel Braddock could do was send out regular patrols to visit settlements and farms in the region, so that Jacinto would know that he couldn't have free rein. But it was largely a futile exercise. Often settlements or farms would be attacked hours after a patrol departed, as if Jacinto were taunting Colonel Braddock, telling him in a roundabout way that his Army was a joke.

Local citizens had complained to Washington, and reinforcements were on the way, according to the scuttlebutt. But the reinforcements hadn't arrived yet, and Colonel Braddock had to make do with what he had. It was a frustrating thankless job. If he'd been stationed in the east, he'd probably be a general by now, but instead he was stuck on a remote outpost in the most dangerous and desolate part of the frontier, and he'd probably be a colonel till he died.

There was a knock on his door, and he recalled his nine o'clock meeting with Lieutenant Lowell, one of the young officers in his command, but young Lowell was having marital problems according to post gossip.

"Come in!" said Colonel Braddock.

The door opened and Lieutenant Lowell entered, holding his hat under his arm and his leather portfolio in his hand. He marched toward the desk and saluted stiffly.

"Lieutenant Lowell reporting, sir!"

"Have a seat, Lieutenant. Smoke if you want to."

Lieutenant Lowell sat on a leather upholstered chair in front of Colonel Braddock's desk and took the papers out of his portfolio. He sat erectly and proceeded to deliver his report, describing farms and settlements visited, territory covered, and so on. Finally he told of how he and his command had stumbled upon John Stone in the desert.

"I spoke with him as we rode back to Santa Maria del Pueblo, and found out he was a West Point graduate who served under Jeb Stuart and Wade Hampton during the war. He'd achieved the rank of captain and commanded a troop."

Colonel Braddock filled his favorite briar with tobacco and lit it, his head wreathed in billows of blue smoke. It seemed that the frontier was full of former Civil War officers. One was constantly bumping into them. Some had recovered nicely from the war and were systematically rebuilding their lives, while others wandered aimlessly from place to place, unable to adjust to civilian life.

"Perhaps we should invite him to dinner some night at the Officers' Club," Colonel Braddock said. "Perhaps he knows some of the men here."

"He does, sir. Sergeant McFeeley of Troop C served under him, but I'm afraid we can't invite Captain Stone to dinner, and that's what I wanted to speak with you about. Sergeant McFeeley visited me at my home first thing this morning and told me Captain Stone got in trouble last night at La Rosita. Seems he killed a Mexican outlaw named Rodrigo Vargas, and now Vargas's bandits are after him. Captain Stone was wounded badly in the fight, and evidently is on his way to Tucson. I was wondering if I could take out a patrol and see if I could find him."

"The Army isn't supposed to involve itself in civilian activity," Colonel Braddock said.

"We patrol constantly, sir. This would be just another patrol, but it might help a brother officer."

The mention of *brother officer* touched a deep chord in Colonel Braddock. He believed in the Officer Corps and the allegiance that all officers should have to each other, particularly if they had gone to West Point.

"How soon can you leave?" Colonel Braddock asked.

"This afternoon, and there's one more favor that I'd like to ask, sir, if you don't mind. Could Sergeant McFeeley be transferred temporarily to my command? He's most anxious about the welfare of Captain Stone, as I told you."

"Tell Sergeant Cowper to draft an order to that effect on your way out." Colonel Braddock puffed his pipe thoughtfully as he looked at Lieutenant Lowell. "I know you've gone on many patrols in the past, Lieutenant, and I know you're an experienced officer, but I feel compelled to tell you to be careful anyway." He picked up Captain Poole's intelligence report. "Jacinto's Apaches are on the warpath as you know, and they've been stepping up their campaign against settlers and any other poor bastard they might find on the desert. Beware of ambush. Watch your flanks and utilize your scouts to the maximum. Remember that knowledge of terrain is sixty percent of any battle. Stay alert, and if you engage the Apache, fight aggressively, because that's the only language he respects. Is that clear?"

"Yes, sir."

"Good luck to you, Lieutenant."

Lieutenant Lowell snapped to attention and saluted. "Thank you, sir."

Stone opened his eyes and saw a red flower on the green arm of a saguaro cactus above him. Past the flower was the clear blue sky. He was aware of a terrible pain in his left shoulder, and his chest stung from one side to the other. He raised his head and saw Juanita sitting on the ground, watching a small animal roasting over a fire that gave off no smoke. In the distance were jagged buttes standing like grotesque towers of Babel.

Juanita noticed him. "How do you feel?"

"Not so good."

"You are the craziest gringo I ever saw in my life, and I have seen many crazy gringos."

"I wouldn't argue with you about that. Could you roll me a cigarette?"

She got to her feet and walked toward him, still wearing the high heels and jewelry she'd been wearing in La Rosita. She looked like a strange mirage arising out of the desert sand.

She knelt beside him, took out his bag of tobacco, and rolled the cigarette.

"How did I get here?" he asked.

"Lobo and I brought you, but mostly Lobo. We had to get out of town *rápido*, before Rodrigo's men came."

"Where are we?"

"How should I know? Ask the Indian."

"Where is he?"

"Somewhere out there. He keeps coming and going back, and every time he comes back he brings something. He is so quiet I cannot even hear him. I don't see him until he is right on top of me. He scares me. Open your mouth."

He opened his mouth and she stuck the cigarette in. Then she lit the end with a match. Stone held the cigarette with his right hand and puffed it to life.

"You are a very crazy man," she said. "I knew it from the

moment I first set eyes on you in church. You are the kind of person who does not understand nothing. How can you get into a fight with a man like Rodrigo? Don't you know that such a man would have friends?"

"To hell with his friends."

"You see what I mean? A man like that—you stay away from him. If it was not for the Indian, you would be dead right now. You are a very *estúpido* man, but also a very brave and good one." She smiled and touched his forehead. "I will take care of you and make you well. Nobody has ever dare stand up to Rodrigo before for me, but you did. I never forget. You have save my life."

"You don't owe me anything," Stone told her. "I don't like people like Rodrigo. They rub me the wrong way."

"Let me tell you something," she said. "Every day I go to church and pray that Santa Maria will free me from Rodrigo. Then, today, I go to church and see you. I think to myself: *Juanita, that is an especial man there. God will answer his prayers.*"

"Now I'm lying on the desert with a bullet in my arm. I wouldn't exactly call that an answer to my prayers."

"You are very lucky to be alive, and you don't have the bullet in your arm anymore. The Indian took it out with his knife. He boil some leaves and put them on your wound. Anyway, I pray to Santa Maria that she will free me from Rodrigo, and a little while later Rodrigo is dead."

"Maybe Santa Maria answered your prayers, but she certainly didn't answer mine."

"How do you know she won't? You are an *estúpido* gringo. You do not understand Santa Maria. Sometimes she helps you right away, like with me at La Rosita, and other times you might have to wait awhile."

Stone placed his cigarette in his mouth and opened his shirt pocket, taking out the picture of Marie. The frame was slightly dented, but otherwise was intact. He looked at Marie for a few seconds, then put the picture back into his shirt. He'd been concerned that the photograph might've been damaged or lost in the fight.

"I do not think she is so pretty," Juanita said.

Suddenly she screamed, raising her hand to her breast. Stone turned around and saw Lobo beside him, carrying wood under one arm and a cloth bag in his hand.

"Do you think you can ride?" he asked Stone.

"If I had to."

"Tomorrow at sunrise we will move on."

"Where are we?"

"On the way to Tucson."

"I thought you said you wouldn't take me."

"I change my mind."

"Thanks for helping me out back there in the saloon. I guess you saved my life."

"You are a fool."

"You see?" said Juanita. "He says the same thing I do. There is something wrong with you. You cannot fight the whole world all by yourself."

Lobo dropped the wood to the ground. Then he opened the top of the sack, revealing a variety of berries. "Food," he said.

"What happened after I passed out?" Stone asked.

Juanita answered: "The Indian stole a few horses and we rode away."

"I don't understand why we had to leave," Stone said. "I didn't do anything wrong. The man attacked me with a knife, and I defended myself."

Juanita shook her head impatiently. "You do not understand, gringo. Rodrigo's men want to kill you."

"What about the law?"

"The sheriff is only one man. Rodrigo's men are many."

"Why doesn't the Army do something?"

Lobo answered: "The bluecoats fight the Apache, and that is all. The bluecoats are not sheriffs."

Stone leaned back on the saddle he was using for a pillow. It was the lawlessness of the frontier all over again. Everybody was drunk, everybody carried at least one gun, thieves and murderers were everywhere, and law was scarce.

"Everything be all right in Tucson," Juanita said. "I get a job in a cantina, and I take care of you. The Indian goes back to his job in the Army. Rodrigo's men find somebody else to kill."

"I still don't think we had to leave," Stone said. "I know one of the officers at Fort Kimball, and I'm a former officer myself. The Army would take care of me."

"Maybe for a while," Juanita said, "but sooner or later you leave Fort Kimball, and then Rodrigo's men get you. You do not understand the kind of people they are. They are very bad hombres and they know how to wait."

Juanita sat beside the fire and turned over the rabbit. Lobo walked toward Stone and kneeled beside him. He reached beside Stone and picked up Stone's two gunbelts. "Your guns are here." He lifted Stone's boot. "Here is your knife."

"Do you expect trouble?"

"Is best to stay ready." He placed his hand on Stone's right shoulder. "You are true warrior. I thought he had you. He cut you many times. But you kill him. Your fight was beautiful."

As the morning sun rose higher in the sky, eighteen Mexican bandits rode in a single column across the desert. Miguel sat on his horse about fifty yards ahead of the rest, acting as scout, studying the ground in front of him, raising his head to the tops of hills, watching for Apaches constantly.

The other Mexicans also were alert, glancing around them at the terrain as their horses plodded over the sand. They wore dirty white pants and shirts, with bandoliers of ammunition across their chests and wide sombreros on their heads.

Antonio led the main column of Mexicans, and he'd been sick ever since he heard that his brother had been killed at La Rosita. Many times he wanted to let go and cry, but couldn't do that in front of his men. He had to show strength even now in the time of his deepest sorrow.

It still was difficult for him to believe that Rodrigo was dead, and Antonio felt a terrible emptiness. Rodrigo had been with him all his life, guiding him, teaching him, and protecting him. Now Rodrigo was gone, killed by a gringo in a knife fight.

Antonio had seen Rodrigo fight with knives before, and there'd been no one quicker or more deadly. Antonio had thought Rodrigo invincible with a knife, and Rodrigo actually *liked* to fight with knives. All the *bandidos* were afraid of him, while Rodrigo had never been afraid of anyone, and now Rodrigo was dead, buried on the desert with a cross made of two branches tied together to mark his grave.

Antonio had no intention of fighting the gringo with a knife when he found him. Antonio intended to shoot him on sight, and afterward maybe work on him with a knife, cut him into little pieces, and feed him to the cucarachas.

Ahead, he saw Miguel raise his arm in the air. Miguel had stopped his horse; evidently he'd seen something. Antonio watched Miguel climb down from his horse, drop to one knee, and study something on the ground.

Antonio and the rest of the column caught up with Miguel. "What is it?" Antonio asked.

"Apaches," Miguel replied.

Antonio climbed down from his horse and looked at the tracks. A large number of unshod horses had passed by within the past few hours.

"How many would you say?" Antonio asked.

"A large war party, maybe thirty."

Antonio took off his sombrero and wiped his forehead with the back of his arm. He and his men wouldn't stand much of a chance against thirty Apache warriors, and Apaches loved to kill Mexicans even more than they loved to kill gringos, due to the many massacres the Mexican cavalry had perpetrated against Apache villages.

Miguel arose and approached Antonio, looking him in the eyes. "I think we should go back, Antonio. This is not a good time to be here."

"Go back if you want to," Antonio told him coldly.

"I understand how you feel, Antonio. Rodrigo was your brother and you loved him very *mucho*. But the desert is dangerous today. The Apaches are on the warpath."

"I am on the warpath too," Antonio replied. "I am not afraid of Apaches. If you want to go back, that is your decision to make. I go on to Tucson to find the killer of my brother, but let me ask you something, Miguel. If you were the one who had been killed by the gringo, do you think Rodrigo would be afraid to go to Tucson to avenge your death?"

Miguel was the oldest member of the band, fifty-three years old, and his mustache and sideburns were streaked with gray. "I will ride with you, Antonio," he said.

Antonio turned around and faced the others. "Anyone else who wants to turn back, to hide with the women?"

Their eyes were downcast, and no one said anything. Miguel climbed onto his horse and rode forward, to take the scouting position once again. Antonio waited until Miguel was fifty yards ahead of him, then raised his hand high over his head and then swept it forward.

The column of Mexican bandits advanced over the trail left by the Apache war party, and continued on its way to Tucson.

Lieutenant Lowell walked into his house and took off his campaign hat. "Samantha?"

There was no answer. Their Mexican maid, Carmen, came out of the kitchen. She was in her twenties with her long black hair worn in pigtails. "She is sleeping," she said softly, one finger over her mouth.

Lieutenant Lowell entered the bedroom and saw Samantha sleeping on top of the bedspread, wearing only a thin gown that had risen high above her thighs, showing her long lissome legs dotted here and there with freckles.

He felt a rise of desire for her. She was so beautiful with her pale complexion and slim body. He didn't want to wake her up, but felt he had to say good-bye to her.

He touched his hand to her shoulder. "Samantha?"

She opened big blue eyes, smiled sleepily, and raised her arms. He dropped on top of her and touched his lips to hers, feeling her firm young body and ripe breasts beneath him.

"I was just dreaming about you," she whispered.

She pulled him against her and kissed him again. They squirmed against each other, kissing and breathing heavily.

"This is such a pleasant surprise," she murmured. "I wasn't expecting you."

"I can't stay long," he replied. "I'm going out on patrol."

She stiffened underneath him, and suddenly the mood in the bedroom changed.

"You just came back from patrol," she said, pushing him away. "How come you're going out again?"

"Apaches are on the warpath."

"They're always on the warpath. There's nothing new about that."

"Colonel Braddock wants me to see if I can rescue that fellow named John Stone who I told you about this morning."

She narrowed her eyes. "You volunteered for the patrol, didn't you?"

"Yes."

"I thought so." She rolled over and got out of bed, straightening her gown, covering herself up. Then she put on her robe and tied the belt. "So," she said, "you'd rather be out with your troopers than here with me, as usual. Isn't that so?"

"I have a job to do. Captain Stone's life is in danger."

"What about my life?"

"You're in no danger that I can see."

"Maybe not, but I'll tell you one thing, Lieutenant Joshua Lowell. Your marriage is in danger and you don't seem to realize it."

"Do you expect me to resign my commission and stay home with you all day?"

"You can be reassigned to the East Coast if you want to."

"Field command is important in the career of an officer, and that's why I need to be here. If you cared about my career, like the other officers' wives on the post, our marriage would be all right, but instead you're always complaining and I'm getting sick of it."

"Is that so? Well I'm getting sick of it too, what do you think of that?"

"I've got to get going," he said. "I'll talk with you when I get back."

"That's the way you always deal with the problems that we have. You'll talk about them when you get back, but then, as soon as you get back, you go out again, because, damn you, *you're always volunteering for patrols!*"

She stood across from him, her hands on her hips, and looked utterly stunning in her rage. He took a step toward her.

"Get away from me," she said, a deadly tone in her voice.

He came closer and was about to wrap his arms around her waist when she slapped him hard across his face. His instinct was to counterpunch, and he raised his fist, but took a deep breath and stopped himself.

"I think I'd better get going," he said huskily.

"Don't expect me to be here when you get back," she replied.

"I'm tired of arguing with you. If you want to go—then go."

He turned around and walked out of the bedroom, leaving her standing beside the bed, trembling with rage.

"The Indian said to drink this."

Stone opened his eyes and saw Juanita's face above him, her lips curled in a faint smile. She held a tin cup in her hand.

"What is it?" he asked.

"Who in hell knows?"

Stone took the tin cup and drank the bitter fluid. "Tastes terrible."

"He said to drink it all."

Stone gulped it down, then handed the cup back to Juanita.

"How do you feel?" she asked.

He moved his left arm, and the pain seemed to be greatly diminished. "I think I'm better," he said.

"Your color is *mucho* healthier. I think you be all right."

"Where's Lobo?"

"He comes and he goes."

They were in the middle of a thicket, and the sky overhead had a few puffy clouds. A faint wind blew, rustling the leaves and branches. In the distance he could see a purple mountain range.

"How're you doing?" he asked her.

"Sometimes I am glad Rodrigo is dead, and other times I am not so sure. I hated him and I was afraid of him, but he took good care of me. I never miss one meal in all the years I was with Rodrigo, but before him I miss many meals. But I know you will take good care of me. I will not miss any meals with you either, I do not think so."

"Wait a minute, Juanita. I think you've misunderstood something. When we get to Tucson, we're splitting up. You go your way and I go mine. I'm engaged to get married, remember?"

"That is just a game you are playing. That woman is gone and you will never see her again. You have kill Rodrigo, and I was his woman. Now I am your woman. You will understand better when you are recover from your wound, and anyway, Tucson is a long distance away. Maybe we never make it. Maybe the Apaches will get us, or maybe Antonio hunt us down first. Antonio is Rodrigo's little brother, only he is not so little. He will want to kill you, gringo, and me too. I will bet you that he is somewhere out here right now, looking for the both of us."

She opened her mouth to scream, but no sound came out. Stone turned his head and saw Lobo emerge from the desert, carrying his little deerskin bag and some canteens full of water.

"That Indian always scare me so much when he show up like that," she said, placing her hand on her heart.

Lobo kneeled beside Stone and removed the crude bandage made from the matted torn sleeve of Stone's shirt. Then he opened his bag and took out some long thin leaves, placing them on the wound.

"You will be well soon," he said.

Lieutenant Lowell sat on his horse, his saber in its scabbard on his belt, his campaign hat low over his eyes. Before him was his patrol, twenty men armed to the teeth plus two Apache scouts, Tim Connors on his dun, and Sergeant Gerald McFeeley, lined up in two ranks in front of the flagpole.

"All right, men!" Lieutenant Lowell shouted. "You've all been through this before and you know what to do! That's Apache country out there, so keep your eyes open, remember your training, and follow your orders! If we run into the Apache, make every shot count! Stay together and be ready for anything! Sergeant McFeeley—move 'em out!"

Sergeant McFeeley called out the orders, and the two ranks turned left, forming two columns. Lieutenant Lowell galloped to the front, followed by the corporal carrying the guidon, and the patrol followed behind them in a clatter of hoofbeats.

Colonel Braddock watched from the window of his office, holding his hands clasped behind his back. Whenever a patrol went out, he always wondered if it'd come back.

Colonel Braddock's eyes focused on Lieutenant Lowell riding at the head of the column on a spirited horse that pranced and danced as if it knew it was special. Lieutenant Lowell sat erectly in his saddle, his elbows straight down and not flapping foolishly like an inexperienced rider, and Colonel Braddock remembered when he'd been a young officer leading men on patrol. He envied Lieutenant Lowell and wished he could be young again, full of piss and vinegar, but that was all over for him now.

Sighing, he returned to his desk and stuffed his briar with tobacco. *I'm just a high-priced clerk,* he thought. *Just an old man in a fancy uniform.*

High on a mountain overlooking Fort Kimball, Black Bear lay on his stomach and watched the cavalry column move onto the desert. He counted the number of soldiers and scouts, noted that they had no cannon, and watched for a while to determine their direction.

Then he arose and crept back to the fire smoldering beneath the blanket. He gripped the corners of the blanket, then pulled it suddenly off the fire.

A huge billow of smoke rose into the sky over the mountain. Black Bear waited for a few moments, then covered the fire with the blanket again. He waited until the smoke built up beneath the blanket, and removed the blanket once more.

A second bellow of smoke floated into the bright blue sky.

Far away, in a little valley, old Jacinto was constructing a snare out of a thin sapling. Watching him was his five-year-old grandson Perico, attired only in moccasins, a breechclout, and a red bandanna holding his straight black hair in place.

Jacinto was sixty-five years old, wrinkled and gnarled, but still sturdy. He sprinkled some pinyon nuts on the ground near the snare. "This is the bait," he explained. "Bait is the most important part of the trap, because without it the rabbit will not even come near the trap."

"Look, Grandfather!"

The boy pointed to the sky behind Jacinto, who turned and saw puffs of smoke rising above the mountains.

"What does it say, Grandfather?"

"We'd better return to the camp."

"Are the bluecoats coming?"

"Maybe."

The little boy pulled out his knife and stood defiantly with his slender legs spread apart. "Let them come! I am not afraid of them! I will kill them all!"

"This is not a good place to fight, Perico. We are in the open. The best place to fight is where the bluecoats cannot see you, and where the bullets from his guns cannot strike you."

The boy looked around. "What about those rocks over there?"

"That would be better." Jacinto pointed. "Do you see that grove of trees over there?"

The boy shielded his eyes from the sun with his right hand as he looked. "There is water there, is that not so, Grandfather?"

"Yes, but you must never go to cool shade, no matter what. If there are bluecoats around, that is where they will be and you will walk right into them."

The old chief and the little boy moved side by side swiftly over the desert, heading back to their encampment in the hills, while behind them the smoke signals rose higher in the sky.

Antonio and his men gathered in a wide coulee lined with clusters of trees, bushes, and cactuses. They watched the smoke rise from the mountains in the distance.

"What do you think it means?" Antonio asked Miguel.

Miguel shrugged. "I do not know. Maybe they have seen us."

"Those mountains are very far away. How can they see us?"

"I would not put anything past the Apache. They have eyes like the eagles."

Antonio wasn't sure of what to do. Rodrigo usually made the decisions for the band.

Ramon Gonzalez, who had a long thin face, leaned on his saddle horn. "I think we should go back," he said. "It is too dangerous out here."

Antonio looked coldly at him. "If you want to go back, go ahead."

"I think all of us should go back, not just me."

"No," Antonio said. "You go back now. Alone. And when you are there, take your blanket and your woman and leave. If I ever see you again, I will kill you."

"But, Antonio . . ."

"Get going!"

Antonio's face was stern and his mouth was set in a grim line. Ramon didn't budge.

"I have been with your brother for many years," Ramon said. "I have always been loyal. You cannot make me leave now."

"You are the one who wants to go back."

"I said we should all go back. This is Apache country. You do not understand the danger."

"I understand the danger," Antonio told him, "but I am not afraid. You are afraid, because you are a coward. Go, before I kill you."

Ramon's face was disfigured by anger. "I am not a coward."

"I say that you are."

Both men stared at each other as they sat atop their horses. The other bandits urged their horses out of the way.

"I told you to leave," Antonio said, his hand hovering over his pistol.

"I am not going," Ramon replied.

They reached for their pistols and fired within a split second of each other, but Ramon's shot was wild and Antonio's wasn't. A red dot appeared on the front of Ramon's shirt, and Antonio triggered again.

Now two red holes were on Ramon's shirt. Ramon gazed at Antonio with eyes glazing over, and Antonio shot him again. Ramon fell off his horse and dropped to the ground.

Antonio's gun smoked in his hand. "Any other cowards want to go back?" he asked.

No one said anything.

"Felix—take his weapons and his horse."

Felix, short and stout, jumped down from his horse and lifted the revolver from Ramon's lifeless hand. Antonio holstered his pistol and reached for his canteen, taking a sip of water.

He turned to Miguel. "How far to the next water hole?"

"A few miles."

Felix slung Ramon's bandolier over his shoulder and tied the reins of Ramon's horse to his saddle horn. Then he climbed onto his horse again.

"Move out," said Antonio.

The bandits urged their horses forward, leaving behind the body of Ramon Gonzalez bleeding onto the sand.

Juanita watched the puffs of smoke arising from the mountains. She and Lobo sat near the fire, which Lobo had just extinguished, while Stone lay several feet away, sleeping soundly.

"What is the smoke saying?" she asked.

Lobo returned his eyes to the smoke signals. "Bluecoats have left Fort Kimball."

"That is very good. I hope we see them."

"There is much desert here. They might be many miles away. Probably we will not see them."

"Maybe we should put up smoke of our own, to attract them."

"Maybe we attract my people, who will kill you and John Stone, and maybe me too. That is not good idea."

Juanita looked at Lobo's dark features and thought of the atrocities Apaches committed against Mexicans, yet here she was alone on the desert with one of them.

"Do not be afraid of me," he said to her. "I will not hurt you."

"I do not trust you," she said.

"I do not trust you either. You make much trouble. John Stone is hurt because of you."

She didn't reply. It was true. If it hadn't been for her, Rodrigo would not have fought John Stone.

Lobo looked down at the ground. "I am sorry. I should not say that. It was not your fault."

Lobo arose suddenly and walked into the chaparral. In seconds he was gone, leaving Juanita alone with Stone.

Juanita looked at Stone. He'd been sleeping soundly ever since Lobo gave him some tea to drink, made from boiled roots of a plant that Lobo had brought to the campsite.

Juanita arose and walked toward Stone, kneeling beside him. Stone lay on his back with his head on his saddle, his chest rising and falling gently as he breathed. A healthy color was returning to his face. Lobo said he'd be able to ride in the morning.

Juanita crossed herself and said a prayer to the Virgin, asking for her protection and assistance. She felt frightened and alone, and in a few hours it would be dark. Wild animals and snakes were on the desert, as well as Apaches, and she still wasn't sure about Lobo. He was a savage, capable of anything.

If only I had never talked to this crazy gringo, she thought.

The Apache encampment was a scattering of wickiup huts on a plateau surrounded by rolling hills. The wickiups were conical, made of bear grass and other foliage, ranging from eight to fifteen feet in diameter and standing seven or eight feet tall in the center. All faced east.

The encampment couldn't be seen from a distance, because the hills hid it from view. A stream passed nearby, and horses grazed on the plain.

Perico, the little boy, watched as the warriors gathered in front of Jacinto's wickiup. They sat on the ground, carrying rifles or bows and arrows, and waited for Jacinto to come out of his wickiup.

Red Feather the medicine man was among them, with Eagle Claw, Black Bear, Nolga, and Tuchee. The last to arrive was Coyotero, one of Jacinto's sons-in-law and also Perico's stepfather, a leader among the warriors. Coyotero was short and thick across the chest, wearing a breechclout and no pants; his legs were swathed with lumpy muscle.

Perico admired Coyotero and hated him at the same time. Coyotero had stolen many horses, killed many bluecoats, and possessed three wives, whereas most warriors only had one wife. One of Coyotero's wives was Perico's mother, White Cloud, and Coyotero often was cruel to her. That was why Perico didn't like him. Coyotero treated White Cloud like a slave and favored Chata, his first wife, who also tormented White Cloud.

Perico's true hero had been his uncle, Lobo, but Lobo went to work for the bluecoats and was considered a traitor. Perico's father, Zhunosho, had been killed by the white eyes while Perico was still a baby, and Perico didn't remember him at all.

Perico remembered Lobo, who had played with him when he was small and gave him the knife he carried. Lobo had been a great warrior, and some thought he was even greater than Coyotero, but Lobo and Coyotero had been enemies, and one day they had a big fight. It went on for a long time and both cut each other many times, but Coyotero finally won. He could have killed Lobo, but Jacinto intervened. Soon thereafter Lobo went away to work for the bluecoats.

Perico stood beside the wickiup and watched the warriors assemble. They were the great men of the tribe, and Perico knew that someday he'd take his place among them. He wanted to be a great warrior too, but doubted that he could do it. He was afraid he wouldn't be strong, fast, or smart enough. Coyotero never taught him anything, and he had to rely on his grandfather Jacinto for lessons, but Jacinto was chief of the tribe and too busy with his many responsibilities to give much time to Perico, who sometimes was afraid he'd never become a great warrior or even an ordinary warrior, and that would be a disgrace.

He also was afraid he wouldn't become a good hunter, and if he weren't a good hunter, he would starve to death. No woman would live in his wickiup if he weren't a good hunter. Perico didn't sleep well and often stuttered when he was nervous, which was often. He frequently fought with other boys, and felt something serious was wrong with him, that he had a terrible flaw that would ruin his life.

The warriors sat quietly in a circle in front of Jacinto's wickiup, waiting for him to come out. In other parts of the encampment, women prepared food, made or repaired clothes, gathered firewood, cared for little children. The boys Perico's age and older watched the warriors intently, their eyes filled with admiration.

Jacinto emerged from his tent and looked strong and healthy although he was old. His posture was regal, and he still was able to kill white eyes in battle.

He took his place in the circle and sat down, crossing his legs. He closed his eyes for a few moments, praying to Yusn, the Great Mystery, then reopened his eyes and said to the gathered warriors:

"I have heard your thoughts even as I sat in my wickiup. I know what you want to do. You want to attack the bluecoats who have come onto our land, and you want to kill them all. But I say to you: you will never kill them all. Whenever we have killed bluecoats, more bluecoats have come. There will always be more bluecoats. And they will never leave us alone, just as the coyote will never leave the deer alone, or the birds will never leave the flowers alone, or the vultures will never leave a carcass alone. Whenever there is blood, there is always more blood. I am sick of so much blood. It has never done any good. Someday we may have to fight bluecoats again, but today there is no reason. That is what I say. That is what I think."

There was silence for a few seconds, and then most of the warriors turned to Coyotero, because they knew he wouldn't agree with Jacinto, and would present the opposite side of the argument.

Coyotero opened his mouth to speak. "We respect the words of Jacinto," he said. "We all know that he has the best interests of our people foremost in his mind. We also know that he has been right about many things in the past, and we respect his wisdom. But I think he is wrong. I think we should kill the bluecoats wherever we find them." He pulled out his knife and held it point up in the air. "This is all the bluecoats understand." He held up his rifle. "And this. It is true, as Jacinto says, that there are many bluecoats, many more than we, but that doesn't mean we should let them pass through our country unharmed. We must fight them wherever we find them. We must kill them whenever we can. It is better to die fighting than run like dogs and hope the bluecoats will leave us alone. The bluecoats will never leave us alone. So let us not be fooled by that argument. I say we must attack and kill these bluecoats who are riding into our country, and if we die, we will die like warriors."

Coyotero paused and looked at the faces of the warriors in the circle, then he continued. "No matter what we do, more bluecoats will keep coming into our country. If we kill these bluecoats now, or if we don't kill them now, more bluecoats will come. This is the way it always has been and this is the way it always will be. All we can do is fight. Bluecoats must know that when they ride into our country, they are riding into their graves."

Coyotero's face was flushed with emotion when he finished speaking. With abrupt angry movements, he lay his rifle on the ground in front of him and jabbed his knife back into the sheath on his belt.

Jacinto spoke again: "Coyotero is a great warrior and he always wants to fight, but I am an old man and I have seen enough fighting. We have all killed many bluecoats, and are we any safer? No, we are less safe than ever. I have been pondering this for some time now, and I believe we must make peace with the bluecoats. I do not know exactly how to do this, but we must begin by stopping the killing. That is the first step."

Coyotero snorted derisively. "What kind of solution is that? We must stop killing them, but it's all right for them to keep killing us? That is madness. Jacinto is a great chief and a great warrior, but I think he no longer understands our situation. There can be no peace with the white eyes until they are dead or we are dead. This small group of bluecoats will not be difficult for us. I say we should wipe them out tomorrow."

Jacinto looked around the circle, and could see that most of the warriors agreed with Coyotero. They had hot blood, like Coyotero, and wanted to kill bluecoats, regardless of the consequences.

"If this is what you want to do, I will not stop you," Jacinto said. "Who knows—maybe you are right and I am wrong. But before you put on your war paint, you must seek the counsel of Red Feather."

Everyone turned to Red Feather, the medicine man, who closed his eyes, turned down the corners of his mouth, and shook his head slowly, indicating that the mountain spirits had told him not to attack the bluecoats. Jacinto arose and walked back to his wickiup, bending low and going inside, pulling the flap over the entrance. Red Feather stood and walked off toward his wickiup, leaving Coyotero with the other warriors.

Coyotero tried to masquerade his resentment. Sometimes he thought Red Feather was a fraud, other times he thought the mountain spirits talked to him. "Red Feather has told us the time is not right for us to kill these bluecoats," he said, "but that does not mean we can't kill other white eyes. Come—let us think of what we can do."

Coyotero got to his feet and walked toward his wickiup. The other warriors followed him, and Perico ran toward Jacinto's wickiup, pushing aside the flap and going inside.

He saw Jacinto lying on his mat. "Are you all right, Grandfather?" he asked.

"I am tired, Perico."

"Red Feather sided with you. That means you were right."

"Only this time. Coyotero wants to kill white eyes, and nothing will stop him."

Perico pulled out his knife. "I hate white eyes too, Grandfather. I want to kill them too."

"Leave me," Jacinto said. "I want to sleep."

Perico sheathed his knife and retreated out of Jacinto's wickiup, leaving Jacinto alone. Jacinto looked at the twigs and branches that comprised the roof of the wickiup. *I can't control them any longer,* he thought, *and soon I will be dead. What will happen to the people then?*

Jacinto closed his eyes and tried to sleep. Against his eyelids, he saw the desert covered with blood.

Samantha had a few drinks of bourbon before going to bed that night. She sat alone in her living room and sipped the whiskey in the light of a coal-oil lamp, while through her open window she heard the sounds of the desert, the night birds and coyotes howling for mates, the hooting of owls, the neighing of horses in the corral.

She felt isolated in a place she hated, as though her life were over even though she was only twenty years old. In Boston she'd had many friends and much to do. There'd been parties, concerts, walks on the Common and lots of friends to talk with, an endless round of enjoyable activities, and men had always clustered around her like bees to honey.

She'd selected Joshua Lowell because he'd looked so dashing and splendid in his West Point uniform. Her girlfriends all wound up with men she considered ordinary, lawyers and doctors and accountants, but she'd have a life of adventure as the wife of an Army officer, and travel to far-off parts of the country, and see interesting things.

She'd been the center of attention when she told her friends she was going to the Arizona Territory. It all sounded so romantic and exotic. But now that she'd been in the Arizona Territory for over a year, she was going crazy.

There was nothing romantic about the desert. It was an ugly barren place and she didn't dare explore it, even if she wanted to, for fear of being murdered by Apaches.

Santa Maria del Pueblo wasn't much either, a dirty little town full of superstitious Mexicans who liked to fight with guns and knives. The restaurants were disgusting and the food unpalatable. Beggars were everywhere, and there was no social life.

The fort didn't provide much either. Most of the officers' wives were frontier women without refinement or culture.

Their primary topics of conversation were their children and the Army. They all acted as if they were *grande dames*, but they were country bumpkins as far as Samantha was concerned. She hated them all.

Her only companion was her husband, but he was away most of the time. He seemed to love his career more than he loved her. *Maybe I should leave him,* she thought, as the whiskey made her feel light-headed. *Maybe I should go back to Boston and get a divorce.*

A tear came to her eye and she brushed it away. If only there were somebody she could talk with. She was thousands of miles from home, in an ugly little house made of mud and straw, and felt like a rat in a trap.

She was getting sleepy; it was time to go to bed. Arising, she walked to the bedroom and washed her face and hands. Then she removed her clothes.

Naked, she stood in front of the mirror and looked at herself in the light of the coal-oil lamp. She thought she was losing her youth and beauty, becoming an old lady. Her skin was pale and her breasts were starting to sag. She was becoming gaunt, and her legs were losing their suppleness.

No wonder he doesn't care about me anymore, she thought sadly. She dropped her nightgown over her fantastic body and blew out the coal-oil lamp, crawling into bed.

A breeze fluttered the curtains, and tears rolled down her cheeks. She'd been so happy back in Boston; maybe she should've married one of those businessmen who'd courted her. They weren't as dashing as Joshua, but they could've given her a decent life, in contrast to the crushing boredom and isolation of Fort Kimball. Anything would be better than this.

A terrible loneliness gnawed inside her, and she rolled over, hugging her pillow tightly, but the pillow was cold and shapeless; it didn't provide the comfort and solace she needed.

She'd heard stories of Apaches who sneaked into people's homes and killed them while they slept. Her tears soaked into the pillow. *I can't stand this any longer. I'm too young to waste my life this way.*

The cavalry patrol camped for the night in a valley next to a stream of water. Tents were pitched, guards posted, and the dinner meal of salt pork and hard tack was prepared.

The largest tent was Lieutenant Lowell's. It had an office in front, with a portable desk and chair, plus a small sleeping area in back, with a cot. Lieutenant Lowell was the only member of the patrol who wouldn't sleep on the ground that night.

Lieutenant Lowell sat on his chair in front of the tent, puffing his cigar, feeling at peace with himself and the world. The patrol had gone smoothly so far and there'd been no problems. They hadn't found any trace of John Stone, but maybe tomorrow they'd pick up his trail.

Lieutenant Lowell looked up at myriads of stars scattered across the sky. The atmosphere was so clear he could see the mountains of the moon, which was full, bright, and bathed the desert in a pale glow, illuminating the tall saguaro cactuses surrounding the campsite.

He heard the sounds of a military camp in the field. Pots and pans clattered, men sang old Army songs around campfires, other men cleaned their rifles. Occasionally a sergeant barked a command.

Lieutenant Lowell wouldn't have traded that moment for anything else in the world. He loved the Army and all it stood for, and loved to be in command.

Back at the post, he was only another low-ranking officer, but here in the field, he was the commanding officer. Everyone deferred to him. His word was law. He saw himself in the tradition of great American military commanders such as George Washington, Andrew Jackson, Winfield Scott, Ulysses S. Grant, Philip Sheridan, and even Stonewall Jackson and Robert E. Lee, the Confederate commanders whose generalship had been so brilliant during the Civil War.

Lieutenant Lowell took a deep breath, inhaling the fragrant desert air. It was wonderful to be in command of fighting men. He wished he could win a great victory against the Apaches. Then Washington would take notice of him, and his career would be made.

He was an avid reader of newspapers, and knew many unknown low-ranking officers like himself had become famous because they'd defeated Indians in battle. It was the best way to win decorations and promotions, and maybe the only way. Since his arrival in Arizona, he'd been in a few skirmishes with Apaches, but nothing big. Somehow he had to find a sizable number of Apaches and wipe them out.

He didn't know exactly how to accomplish that. Luck had a lot to do with it. But he was ready for the confrontation, and indeed looked forward to it. He knew all the latest theories of war, tactics, and strategies. His men had superior weaponry to the Apaches. All he needed was the opportunity to prove himself.

A figure approached out of the darkness. It was Sergeant Gerald McFeeley, who came to attention in front of Lieutenant Lowell and saluted. "The perimeter is secure, sir. I just checked it myself."

"Have a seat, Sergeant. You may smoke if you like."

Sergeant McFeeley sat on the folding chair beside Lieutenant Lowell and rolled a cigarette, lighting it with a match. "I been thinkin', sir," he said. "It appears that Cap'n Stone ain't stickin' to the main trails, so maybe we ought to move straightaway into the desert tomorrow. I figger he's movin' west, so maybe we should sweep north and south, and see if we can cut his trail."

"Sounds like it's worth a try, Sergeant."

The two men smoked in silence, staring across the campsite and into the desert beyond it. Insects chirped around them. A soldier walked past Lieutenant Lowell's tent, carrying an armload of firewood.

Lieutenant Lowell turned to Sergeant McFeeley. "It might be helpful if I knew a bit more about Captain Stone. You served with him in the war. What kind of officer was he?"

Sergeant McFeeley leaned back in his chair and crossed his legs. "Well, he wasn't much of a talker, and he wasn't the friendliest officer I ever seen, but all the men liked him and I did too. He always made sure we had enough to eat, and when food was short, he fought for us to make sure we got our fair share. He never asked us to do anything he wouldn't do himself, and when we went into a fight, he was always up front, leadin' the way instead of hidin' in the rear like some officers. He was the strongest man I ever seen, and he was steady under fire. Old Wade Hampton liked him a lot. They was neighbors back home in South Carolina before the war."

Lieutenant Lowell knew who Wade Hampton was. With no military experience whatever, he'd formed the Hampton Legion at his own expense and was commissioned a colonel of cavalry. He was one of the southerners who opposed the secession, just like Robert E. Lee, but fought for the Confederacy anyway, eventually rising to the rank of major general and becoming commander of the Confederate Cavalry Corps.

"Did you know Captain Stone well?" Lieutenant Lowell asked.

"Not that well, sir. We was never friends. But we got on all right together. He was a good officer, and I couldn't say more about any man."

"You've served under him, so you must know something about the way his mind works. He's out here someplace, wounded, traveling with an Apache Indian and a Mexican woman. What do you think he'll do?"

"Exactly the opposite of what you think he'll do, sir. I wouldn't put anything past him."

Later, sitting alone in front of his tent, Lieutenant Lowell pondered what Sergeant McFeeley had told him. Lieutenant Lowell couldn't help feeling inferior to Captain Stone, because he knew his men didn't respect him the way Sergeant McFeeley respected Captain Stone. Lieutenant Lowell knew that three or four years down the road, the men who were serving under him now wouldn't praise him and call him an outstanding officer. It'd be a miracle if they even remembered who he was.

He wondered what qualities an officer had to have in order to inspire loyalty. He'd known officers who were conscientious and decent, but who were held in contempt by their men, and other officers, such as Colonel Braddock, also conscientious and decent, who were much admired by the men.

Lieutenant Lowell wanted to be a great officer and be loved by his men, but didn't know how to go about it. He suspected it would all come together if he could win a great victory against the Apaches. The men respected fighting skill—that much was clear to him. Lieutenant Lowell hoped he'd be steady under fire and a brave fighter when the time came to charge, and he hoped that time would be soon.

If only I could find Jacinto's camp, he thought.

4

"TIME TO GET up," said Lobo.

Stone opened his eyes. It was still dark, the dawn a faint glimmer on the horizon. Lobo moved toward Juanita, who was rolling up her blanket. Lobo threw the bags of food he'd collected over his horse.

Stone's shoulder didn't hurt as much as yesterday, and he felt much stronger. He sat up and pulled on his boots, inserting his knife in its sheath. Standing, he strapped on his gunbelts, then walked to Lobo and Juanita who were kneeling by the fire pit.

The fire hadn't been lit, because the flames could be seen a long distance in the dark. Lobo passed Stone a haunch of cooked rabbit.

"Eat it all," Lobo commanded.

Stone bit off a chunk of the meat and was surprised that it was so tender and juicy. Lobo placed a bag full of berries between them, and Juanita took a handful. Canteens full of water were close by.

They ate silently as dawn brightened the horizon, casting long shadows around them, silhouetting mountains and buttes in the distance. Stone was surprised by how well he felt. The weakness of yesterday was nearly gone.

But as he reached for the berries, a sharp pain shot through his shoulder, and he winced.

"Easy," said Lobo. "Do not push yourself too hard." He handed Stone a root. "Eat some of this."

Stone bit into it, and it was sweet as sugar. "What is it?"

"Just a plant."

"I guess there's food all around us, if you know where to look."

"That is so," Lobo said. "White eyes doesn't know where to look. That's why white eyes must bring his whole kitchen with him whenever he comes to the desert."

"You don't like white people much."

"I hate white eyes."

"Why are you helping us?"

"Because you are a warrior, and she is your woman."

"She's not my woman. Another woman is my woman."

Lobo laughed. Stone looked at Juanita, and she stared back at him.

"You see?" she asked.

"I don't see anything."

"That's because you are a dumb gringo."

Stone chewed some berries. He was alone on the desert with an Apache who hated white people and a Mexican who thought he was a dumb gringo. Bloodthirsty Mexican bandits were following him, and the desert was crawling with Apaches who loved to torture white people.

"How far to Tucson?" he asked.

"Two, three days," Lobo said. "Depends on whether we have any trouble."

They finished breakfast and Lobo loaded the horses with supplies.

"Saddle up," said Lobo. "You take that one," he told Stone.

Stone walked toward the horse, a chestnut gelding with sad eyes, and climbed into the saddle, feeling a sharp pain down his side.

"Do not worry," Lobo said. "You will get stronger every day."

Juanita placed one foot in the stirrup and swung her other leg around, her dress riding up over her knee. She'd combed her hair with her fingers and washed her face earlier in the

morning, and her breasts pushed against the front of her blouse.
She looked like a wild she-creature of the desert.

Lobo mounted his horse and turned to the others. "Be quiet.
Do what I say, and do not ask questions. Let us go."

Lobo prodded the flanks of his horse with his heels, and
the horse moved forward. Juanita went second, and Stone was
last. The three rode off into the chaparral as the sun rose in
the sky.

Coyotero sat in his wickiup, holding up a tin mirror. Carefully,
with a steady hand, he painted a red stripe from his left ear,
across his nose and cheeks, to his right ear.

Perico poked his head into the wickiup and saw what Coyotero was doing. "Are you going to war, Stepfather?"

"Get away from me."

Perico pulled his head out of the wickiup and ran to the one
where he lived with his mother. He entered it and let loose
the tears.

His mother sat in the middle of the wickiup, shelling pinyon
nuts. "What is wrong, Perico?" she asked.

Perico cried, his frail body wracked with sobs. She placed
her arm around his shoulders. "Don't cry, baby," she cooed.
"I will always love you."

Roughly he pushed her away, leaping to another part of the
wickiup where he could be alone. "I will be a great warrior someday!" he said to her. "I do not need anybody to love me!"

Meanwhile, a crowd of warriors had gathered in front of
Coyotero's wickiup, waiting for him to come out. Their faces
were painted and they were ready for war. Each wore a Medicine Cord, a loosely braided sash of two hide strings twisted
around each other and draped across the body from the right
shoulder to the left side. A small bag of pollen hung from each
Medicine Cord. The combination was supposed to provide luck
and protection in serious danger.

Coyotero emerged from his wickiup, carrying his rifle. He
looked at the others, then turned and walked toward Jacinto's
wickiup. The other warriors followed him. The women and
children watched them go, wondering what their plans were.
The camp had been in a state of tension ever since the big
meeting yesterday.

Coyotero came to Jacinto's wickiup. "Jacinto!" he shouted. "We have come to speak with you."

Inside the wickiup, Jacinto was sleeping. He sat up, rubbed his eyes, and wondered what was going on. Coyotero was hollering his name as if Jacinto were a common warrior, instead of a chief.

Jacinto stepped out of his wickiup and found himself in front of Coyotero and the other warriors, painted and armed for combat. Jacinto drew himself to his full height, which was a few inches taller than Coyotero.

"What do you want?" Jacinto asked.

"We have come to tell you that we are going after horses."

"We have had no meeting to discuss this."

"I have discussed it with them," Coyotero replied, indicating the warriors behind him. "We need horses. I saw no need of a meeting. This is not like making war against the bluecoats."

Coyotero always was making inroads on Jacinto's authority. Coyotero sought to depose him, that was clear, and there wasn't much Jacinto could do about it.

"Where is your medicine man?" Jacinto asked. "How can you go on a raid without a medicine man?"

Coyotero had no great faith in medicine men, and didn't want a medicine man meddling with his plans, but most of his warriors did have faith in them. Coyotero had hoped to avoid the issue, but Jacinto had raised it in order to assert himself in some small way.

"It is not such a big raid," Coyotero said sullenly. "I did not think it necessary to seek out the counsel of Red Feather."

"That is an affront to the mountain spirits," Jacinto replied. "It is like saying that they do not matter. Woe to the warrior who does not respect the mountain spirits. Every warrior needs their aid. You must take Red Feather with you."

Coyotero heard his warriors murmuring behind him, and they were agreeing with Jacinto. Coyotero felt himself being backed into a corner.

"Very well," he said to Jacinto. "I accept your wise counsel as always. I will take Red Feather with us."

Jacinto raised his hand in the air. "May Yusn give success to your raid."

• • •

Lobo, Juanita, and Stone rode across the desert, staying out of open spaces, hugging the shadows of mountains, and moving through regions of thick foliage.

Stone had been wounded before, and had never recovered so rapidly. He could even move his left arm fairly well. His head was clear and he felt wide awake. He believed he could fight if it were necessary.

It was two or three days to Tucson, Lobo had said. They had a lot of desert to cover, and it was Apache country. Stone pulled out the Colt in the holster on his right, felt the balance, and dropped it back into the holster.

If Apaches attacked, he'd be ready for them. He looked around warily. In Nolan they'd told him he could stare directly at an Apache and not see him, because Apaches were masters at camouflaging themselves on the desert.

Stone adjusted his hat on his head, to keep the rising sun out of his eyes. Lobo stood in his stirrups and looked back at Stone, to make sure he was all right. The three of them passed a scattering of saguaro cactuses twenty feet tall, and continued on their way toward Tucson.

Coyotero and his warriors descended a hill not far from their encampment. Before them stretched a basin of gravel and sand, sparsely dotted with bear grass and prickly pear. They gathered around Coyotero, awaiting his orders.

Coyotero's dark skin glistened with sweat, and his bead necklace glittered in the sun. He sat atop a sorrel horse with a white blaze on his forehead. Coyotero's mouth was a thin slash on his face.

"Follow me," he said, wheeling his horse around.

He kicked his horse's ribs with his heels, and his horse moved across the sandy basin. His men followed behind him in a column of twos, and bringing up the rear was Red Feather the medicine man.

Red Feather was annoyed at the lack of respect he was receiving from Coyotero, who had not once asked for Red Feather's advice. It was clear to Red Feather that he had been taken on the raid only because Jacinto insisted upon it, not because Coyotero wanted him.

Red Feather didn't know where they were going or what their plans were. He hadn't been asked to pray to the mountain spirits for assistance and protection, or to divine their will.

Red Feather gazed up at the blue cloudless sky, and it seemed that the spirits were talking to him. They were warning him to proceed cautiously, because disaster lay ahead. For a brief split second he had a vision of flaming wickiups and women and children lying dead on the ground, covered with blood.

A chill passed through him. The vision passed.

He knew it would be pointless to tell Coyotero what he'd seen, because Coyotero would pay no attention. Coyotero had no respect for the old ways.

Red Feather had seen much war. He'd participated in the biggest battle ever fought between Apaches and bluecoats in July of 1862, in Apache Pass. Cochise and Mangas Coloradas had led the Apaches, but the bluecoats had two howitzers. The explosive shells were too much for the Apaches, who were forced from the field, leaving many dead behind, and even Mangas Coloradas himself had been seriously wounded.

Jacinto had been in that fight too, and was shot through the stomach, but survived. Jacinto and Red Feather knew of the power of the bluecoats, and respected it. Coyotero didn't respect it. All he wanted to do was strike back. Such a man would come to a bad end.

Red Feather said nothing of this to any of the warriors in the raiding party. He rode quietly at the rear of the column, covering his nose with his bandanna so he wouldn't have to breathe everybody's dust. Coyotero and many of his warriors had turned their backs on the old Apache life-way, and that meant the mountain spirits would turn their backs on them. Great misfortune lay ahead of them, Red Feather believed. Nothing could be done about it, just as the waters of a great river could never be turned back.

Red Feather felt a great sorrow in his heart. It didn't bother him that the warriors didn't respect him, but they didn't respect the mountain spirits who gave victory to warriors.

What will the mountain spirits do to those who turn their backs on them? he wondered.

•   •   •

As Samantha gradually woke up, she thought she was hugging Josh. She pressed her lips against his, and his lips were dry and formless. Then she realized she was kissing her pillow, and with a cry of rage she came fully awake. She picked up the pillow and flung it across the room.

Sun streamed through the drapes. She didn't have to look outside to know it'd be another clear bright day at Fort Kimball, because every day was clear and bright at Fort Kimball. It'd start getting hot around eleven o'clock, and she'd sweat like a pig until evening, when it became cool again.

It was the same every day. There was no change. How she longed for one of those dark mysterious days when the fog rolled in from Boston harbor and covered everything in a soft gray mist. You could feel it on your cheeks; it was cool and refreshing.

The Arizona sun gave her a headache. She rolled out of bed, blew her hair out of her eyes, and looked around the bedroom.

It was about one fourth the size of her bedroom on Beacon Hill, with no beautiful paintings, no nice furniture, only adobe walls and a wooden plank floor. "I can't take it anymore," she said.

She put on her robe and shuffled to the kitchen to make a pot of coffee, but when she looked at the stove and thought about making a fire, she didn't feel up to it. Instead she returned to the living room, took the bottle of whiskey from the cupboard, and sat on the sofa.

She raised the bottle to her lips and took a sip. The whiskey burned all the way down and made tears come to her eyes. Her husband was never home, and she was nearly twenty-five hundred miles from Boston.

There was a knock on the door, and Samantha hid the bottle behind her. "Come in."

The door opened and Carmen the maid entered, carrying a basket containing the food she'd purchased that morning in the market in Santa Maria del Pueblo.

"I don't need you today," Samantha said. "Go home."

"You are not well, señora?"

"No, I am not well."

"I can make you better, maybe."

"Just go away please. I'll pay you for the food."

Samantha arose and walked to the bedroom to get the money, and Carmen saw the neck of the bottle poking out of the cushions on the sofa. Samantha returned a few moments later and dropped some coins in Carmen's outstretched hand. Carmen smelled the whiskey on Samantha's breath.

"Señora, I am worry about you."

"Worry about yourself and leave me alone," Samantha replied, slamming the door in her face.

Samantha returned to the sofa and collapsed upon it, pulling out the bottle of whiskey and removing the cork.

I don't have anything to live for, she thought. *I might as well become a drunk like everybody else around here.*

Near noon, Lobo raised his hand in the air. Behind him, Juanita and John Stone pulled back on the reins of their horses. They were surrounded by trees, cactuses, and thick underbrush on a vast plateau with a single tall butte in the distance.

Lobo slung his canteen over his shoulders and climbed down from his horse, then walked back to Juanita and Stone.

"Give me your canteens," he said. "I will go for water."

"Why cannot we go too?" Juanita said, perspiration covering her forehead and cheeks. "I would like to take a wash."

"Foolish woman," Lobo replied. "You must stay away from water holes. This is the country of my people. Do you want to die today?"

Juanita tossed him her canteen. Stone drank deeply from his, then handed it to Lobo.

"You two dismount and have a rest," Lobo said. "I will be back soon."

Lobo took two steps backward, turned around, and disappeared into the chaparral. Stone climbed down from his horse and sat in the shade of a cottonwood tree. Juanita joined him, and Stone rolled a cigarette.

"How is your wound?" Juanita asked.

"Much better. Lobo is the best doctor I ever had."

Juanita spat into the sand. "You watch out for him, gringo."

"He saved my life. I don't think he means us any harm."

"Maybe he saved your life so he can kill you himself some other time. And me too. Maybe he is going for his Indian friends right now." She looked from side to side suspiciously. "I do not like it here."

"Lobo will be back soon. We won't be here long." Stone placed his hand on her shoulder. "Don't worry so much. We'll be in Tucson tomorrow maybe, and you'll be singing in the best saloon in town."

"Nothing good ever happens to me," she said. "I am a very unlucky person."

"It does no good to remember bad things."

"I cannot forget them. If I told you what Rodrigo do to me, when I was only a girl, you would be sick."

"You have to look forward to the future, not the past."

"I wish Rodrigo was still alive," she said, "so you could kill him again."

"Maybe next time he'd kill me."

"I do not think so, gringo. You are a good fighter, for a gringo. I wonder how you would do against the Indian."

"Lobo and I are friends," Stone said. "We aren't going to fight each other."

"It is a miracle that you have come this far in life, gringo. I guess it is because you are a good fighter, that you have come so far. Otherwise you would have been in the ground long ago."

As Stone and Juanita spoke softly, Lobo crawled toward the water hole, the three canteens slung over his shoulder. Every few feet he paused and listened, then resumed his movement.

He knew that the water hole was used regularly by his people, and didn't want to take the chance of being seen. The only thing to do was advance silently, fill the canteens quickly, and leave rapidly, covering his tracks.

He thought of John Stone and the Mexican woman, back in the chaparral, and how strange it was that he was helping them. Just a few years ago he would've killed them both on sight, if he saw them on the desert, but that had been before he fought with Coyotero and was banished from the tribe.

Lobo hated Coyotero with all his heart. Coyotero had been the only man who'd ever defeated him in a fight, and Lobo had replayed the fight over and over in his mind ever since, trying to figure out what he'd done wrong, so he'd never do it again.

He still didn't know what it was. Maybe Coyotero had been faster, or smarter, or maybe the mountain spirits had smiled on Coyotero that day, instead of him. It was difficult to see how that could happen, because Coyotero wasn't respectful of the mountain spirits, whereas Lobo always had prayed regularly and participated fully in all the religious rites and observances.

There was a commotion in the bushes in front of Lobo. Wings flapped, followed by a screeching sound, and a large owl launched itself into the air, flying past Lobo.

Lobo went pale with fear. Apaches believed owls were the ghosts of people who'd been wicked in life and continued doing evil after death. When an owl flew past an Apache, it was a sign that someone was going to die.

Lobo's heart pounded, and he fought the rising panic. Who was going to die? he wondered. Was it John Stone, the Mexican woman, or Lobo?

Lobo wished he could go to Red Feather for help, but didn't know where Red Feather was, and couldn't return to the camp anyway. Only a medicine man could fight the Owl Sickness.

Lobo knew he had to keep going, and he couldn't let John Stone and the Mexican woman know what he'd seen. Somehow he had to be a warrior until the end, when he rode the Ghost Pony.

The world had become a different place for Lobo. A few minutes ago he had been confident and strong, whereas now he was plagued with doubt and felt weakened. The Owl Sickness was upon him.

Carmen the maid hesitated before the home where Colonel Braddock lived with his wife. She was afraid she might get in trouble for what she was going to do. A little voice in her head told her to turn around and go back to Santa Maria del Pueblo and forget about what she'd seen, but something made her stay. The truth was she was more afraid of the colonel's wife than she was of the voice in her head.

She knocked on the door. A few seconds later it was opened by Luisa, the Braddocks' maid.

"I would like to speak with Mrs. Braddock, please," Carmen said haltingly. "I think it is very important."

Luisa looked at her coldly, then asked her to enter the vestibule. Carmen stood nervously beside a bright-colored Navaho Indian blanket hung on the wall for decoration. A few minutes later Mrs. Braddock appeared, a tall gray-haired woman wearing a high-necked white blouse and a long white skirt.

"You wanted to see me?" Mrs. Braddock asked with a smile.

Carmen curtsied and bowed her head. "Once you told me, señora, that if I ever had any *problemas*, or saw anything bad, I should come to you first, do you remember?"

"Of course I remember. Come with me, please. Luisa, bring us some tea."

Mrs. Braddock took Carmen's hand and led her across the living room and down a corridor to a small library furnished with a desk and a few chairs.

Both of the women sat. Carmen looked at all the books and felt intimidated, because she was illiterate and feared the knowledge that might be in the books, knowledge that could be used against her.

Mrs. Braddock patted her hand. "What's wrong, my dear?"

Carmen placed one hand on top of the other and squeezed her hands together. "I hope there will be no *problemas*, señora."

"I can't promise you there will be no *problemas*. There are always *problemas* in this world. But the *problemas* may be worse if you don't tell me immediately what's on your mind."

"It is Mrs. Lowell," Carmen said. "She is *mucho* sick." Carmen pointed to her right temple. "Here, in the *cabeza*. She is drinking whiskey *todos los días*. She fight with her husband. Today she tell me to go away. She is drinking right now in the dark like a *borracha*. I think there will be many *problemas*. That is what I have come to tell you."

Mrs. Braddock sat straight in her chair, her hands folded in her lap. "Leave everything to me," she said. "I'll take care of Mrs. Lowell."

Miguel was in a rotten mood, and it was getting worse every moment. The sun was unusually hot and Miguel felt as though he was a tortilla in an oven.

He was angry at Antonio for bringing them out on the desert on such a hot day when they could be back in the cave drinking and smoking and having fun with the women. Maybe they even could've roasted a wild pig.

Miguel was the oldest of all the bandits, and didn't have the energy he used to have. The heat bothered him more than ever. He wished he had sons who could take care of him, but he had no children at all. Women who'd been with him had gone with other men afterward and had children from them, so he knew something was wrong in his *cojones*. He was not a complete man, somehow. Instead of enjoying his old age, he was riding on the desert in the sun.

He saw movement in the corner of his eye and turned his head abruptly in that direction. In the far distance, across a vast stretch of desert, he saw three Apache warriors riding in a direction parallel to the one he and the others were on, but the Apaches didn't appear to notice him.

Miguel dismounted quickly, turned around, and motioned to the others. They climbed down from their horses, and he ran back to them, holding his sombrero on his head so it wouldn't fall off.

"What is wrong?" Antonio asked.

Miguel pointed. "Apaches. Three of them. Headed that way. I don't think they saw us, but maybe they did."

Antonio thought it over. "We'll wait here a little while until they're gone, and then move out again."

"No, Antonio," Miguel replied. "We should not wait here, because if they saw us, they will know where to find us. We must wait someplace else."

Miguel had been traversing the desert all his life and knew the region fairly well. He looked around and saw mountains not far to the south. "There," he said, pointing, "but we must go on foot because it will be more difficult for the Apaches to see us that way."

"We will follow you," Antonio said.

Miguel held his horse by the bridle and led him into the thick chaparral. The others followed, and Antonio glanced furtively behind him, hoping the Apaches hadn't seen them.

Salty perspiration dripped from Lieutenant Lowell's mustache to his lips, and his shirt was plastered to his skin. Behind him he heard the trudging of horses' hooves and the rattling of cavalry equipment. The desert was unbearably hot, and buzzards circled in the sky overhead.

Lieutenant Lowell knew he had to set the example for his men, and sit upright in his saddle, but he felt like crawling into the shade and taking a nap. The sun sapped his energy and made him feel mildly dizzy.

But he sat erectly in his saddle and squared his shoulders as his horse clomped over the desert sand. Ahead, Tim Connors and his Apache scouts were reconnoitering the terrain. In the distance was a range of brown craggy mountains shimmering in the bright sunlight.

Lieutenant Lowell couldn't understand how the Apaches could live and thrive in the desert. It was a hellish climate unfit for human habitation, in his opinion.

"Connors must've seen somethin'," said Sergeant McFeeley, riding next to him.

Lieutenant Lowell raised his eyes and saw Tim Connors riding back toward him at a trot. The old scout's hat brim was pushed back by the windstream, and his thin legs flapped from side to side against the ribs of his horse.

Connors pulled back his reins and his horse slowed down as he approached Lieutenant Lowell.

"Apache tracks," Connors said. "Lots of 'em." He pointed toward the west. "Headed in that direction."

"How many?"

"Thirty or forty."

I wonder what they're up to? Lieutenant Lowell thought. They could be out hunting deer, or they could be on a raid.

"How old are the tracks?"

"An hour or two."

Lieutenant Lowell found himself faced with a dilemma. Should he follow the Apaches and see where they were headed, or continue sweeping through the valley in his search for John Stone?

The patrol moved forward and reached the Apache scouts dismounted beside the tracks. Lieutenant Lowell, Tim Connors, and Sergeant McFeeley climbed down from their horses and joined them.

Lieutenant Lowell dropped to one knee and looked at the tracks. He'd been in Arizona Territory long enough to know what the tracks of unshod horses looked like, and that's what these were.

"I think we should go after them, sir," Connors said. "They're prob'ly up to no good."

Lieutenant Lowell glanced at Sergeant McFeeley, whose face was begging him to continue the search for John Stone. Standing, he took off his campaign hat and ran his fingers through his sweaty black hair. If Apaches were on the prowl in the area, that meant that John Stone, a brother officer, was in serious danger.

"No," said Lieutenant Lowell, "we'll continue on the course we're on. Take the point, Mr. Connors."

Connors nodded to the Apache scouts, and they climbed onto their horses, wheeling them around and heading north again. Lieutenant Lowell and Sergeant McFeeley walked back to their horses and mounted up. Lieutenant Lowell held his reins in his left hand and raised his right arm in the air, moving it forward. The silence of the desert was overcome by the sound of cavalry on the march, and a cloud of dust rose into the air. The patrol crossed the tracks left by unshod ponies and headed north toward the mountains.

John Stone, Juanita, and Lobo rode through a land where rocks sat on the desert like giant clinkers surrounded by forests of yucca, prickly pear, and elephant trees. The sun beat on them fiercely as their horses plodded along, their heads hanging low.

Stone noticed that his horse's gait was becoming irregular, and thought the heat was bothering the animal, but then the horse began to limp. Stone pulled back the reins and climbed down from the saddle to see what was wrong.

Ahead, Lobo heard him stop. Lobo brought his horse to a halt and walked back to see what was wrong with Stone. Juanita took the opportunity to climb down from her saddle and exercise her legs.

Stone examined the hooves of his horse, and saw that half a horseshoe had broken off one of them. "Damn!" he said, and pried the rest of the horseshoe off with his knife, then trimmed the hoof with the blade of the knife so it'd be even.

Lobo watched him. "You not get far without new horseshoe," he said. "I know a place not far away. Follow me."

"A place out here?" Stone asked incredulously. "What is it?"

"A ranch," Lobo replied. "Friends. Come on."

They climbed into their saddles, and Lobo rode off in a southwesterly direction. Juanita and Stone followed, Stone's horse still limping. Stone found himself wondering what kind of ranch could exist in this demanding region of desert.

Must be hardy folk, he thought.

Samantha sat on the sofa, gripping the bottle of whiskey in her right hand. She still wore her nightgown, and the drapes covered all the windows of her home.

She could hear the sounds of the fort outside. Horses galloped by and sergeants shouted orders on the parade field. Occasionally bugles were blown. She heard the laughter of men and the voices of women, and then there were long periods of silence when she felt as if she were all alone in the world.

She felt sick and terrible. An unpleasant odor arose from her body.

She couldn't believe that she'd sunk so low. In Boston she'd been a vivacious young woman with throngs of friends and male suitors coming out of the woodwork. She'd dressed in the latest fashions and never had a hair out of place, and now she was an absolute mess with no volition and no reason to smile.

There was a knock on the door, and she decided not to answer it. She didn't want to see anybody. It couldn't be anything important.

The knock came again, louder this time and more insistent. *If I'm quiet, they'll go away,* Samantha thought.

Then a voice came piercing through the timbers of the door. "Mrs. Lowell!" shouted Martha Braddock. "I know you're in there! Open up!"

Samantha's hair nearly stood on end with fear. She didn't want to see anybody, least of all the colonel's wife! She looked around frantically. What could she do?

Martha Braddock knocked on the door more insistently. "Mrs. Lowell—if you don't open this door right now I'll break it down!"

Samantha swallowed hard. She saw a terrible scandal looming for herself and Josh. Burying the bottle under the cushions of the sofa, she arose, adjusted her hair, and walked unsteadily to the door. There was no escape. She had to do it. Reaching out toward the doorknob, she turned it and opened the door.

The bright sunlight seared her eyeballs, and standing in the middle of the glare was Martha Braddock, wearing a wide straw hat.

"May I come in?" asked Mrs. Braddock.

"Yes, of course," replied Samantha, "but I'm not feeling well, I'm afraid. I hope you'll excuse my appearance."

"Don't worry about that," Mrs. Braddock replied, walking past her and entering the living room. "No wonder you're not feeling well. It's so gloomy in here." She threw open the drapes. "I think you need a cup of coffee. I could use one too."

She entered the kitchen, and Samantha followed like a sick cat. Mrs. Braddock bustled at the stove, stoking the fire, and filled the coffeepot with water. Her movements were decisive, like a soldier.

She boiled the water and prepared the coffee, while Samantha watched silently, thinking she was in deep trouble. Mrs. Braddock was the wife of the commanding officer, and a commanding officer could make or break a young officer's career. Josh took his career seriously, and if it was destroyed by anything Samantha did, there was no telling how he might respond. A terrible scandal could ensue, and there might be reverberations all the way to Beacon Hill.

Mrs. Braddock opened the cupboard and took down cups and saucers. Then she carried the coffeepot and cups and saucers to the living room, placing them on the coffee table.

"Sit down and drink some of this," she commanded.

She poured coffee for Samantha and handed it to her, then poured a cup for herself. She sat on a chair opposite the sofa and Samantha dropped onto the sofa, but as she did so, the bottle of whiskey popped up like a bad dream from between the cushions.

Samantha turned red and pushed it down.

"It's all right," Mrs. Braddock said. "I already saw it. Would you pass it to me, please?"

With trembling hands, Samantha extended the bottle toward Mrs. Braddock, who took it, pulled out the cork, and poured some into her coffee.

"Nothing like a little whiskey once in a while to restore the spirit," Mrs. Braddock said, "but we wouldn't want to use it to excess, would we, Samantha?"

"No, Mrs. Braddock, of course not."

"Call me Martha, please." She looked Samantha up and down, and then her eyes softened. "My dear, you look terrible. I'm sure you feel terrible too. Care to tell me what's bothering you?"

"I'm not feeling well, I'm afraid."

"Would you like me to get Dr. Lantz?"

"Not just yet, I don't think. All I need is some rest."

"I suspect that's not what you need at all. I'd recommend activity, something to do, a focus for your energies. What would you need rest from? You do no work, do you?"

"Actually no."

"I didn't think so. Like the rest of the officers' wives, you have a maid. But while the rest of us engage in a variety of social and charitable activities, you stay home and mope, isn't that correct?"

Samantha wanted to throw the old biddy out on her ear, but Mrs. Braddock was the commanding officer's wife. "I do stay home a lot, Mrs. Braddock."

"I asked you to call me Martha. Let me tell you something. I was once like you, the young wife of a young second lieutenant, and our first post together was in Kansas when it was wild like this. I too was alone and bored, as I imagine you are. I too wanted to return home, to Philadelphia. But I stayed with my husband, and I'm glad I did. I believe I've had a much more interesting and enjoyable life than if I'd remained in Philadelphia going to tea parties every afternoon and discussing the weather. Those people back there don't know what weather is. *This* is weather." Mrs. Braddock pulled a handkerchief from her sleeve and patted the beads of perspiration from her forehead. "Now as I see it, you have two choices. You can go whining back home with your tail between your legs, like a pathetic little puppy, or you can remain with your husband and be a credit to him, your country, and the service. Those were the choices that faced me once, and now they face you. The decision is up to you, and no one can make it for you. But I'm afraid you'll have to make it soon. A small military installation like this one thrives on gossip. Soon everyone will be talking about you. If you want to drag your name down, that's your business, but I don't think you should drag down the young man you're married to. Lieutenant Lowell has the makings of a fine officer, and it would be a tragedy if his career were marred by something you might do."

"I would never do anything to hurt Josh," Samantha said.

"That's nonsense," Mrs. Braddock said. "You've hurt him already by keeping your windows covered throughout the morning. Do you think people wouldn't notice that and think it odd? Look at you—in your nightclothes at one o'clock in the afternoon. This is not the way the wife of an officer behaves. You ought to be ashamed of yourself."

Samantha had never been spoken to this way in her life. She leaned forward on the sofa and said with barely suppressed rage: "I hate Fort Kimball. It's the most boring place I've ever been in my life. There's no one to talk to, nothing to do, nothing to see. I think military life is absolutely ridiculous, all that strutting and posturing, saluting and blowing horns. It would be laughable, were it not so demented."

"Demented?" asked Mrs. Braddock. "You think it's demented? This nation wouldn't exist right now, if it weren't for its soldiers. Boston would be a colonial outpost, instead of the great city that it is, if it weren't for men like the ones who proudly wear the uniform of the United States Army on this post. Military life isn't demented, but you are because you're nothing more than a simpering, whimpering little *snob!*"

Samantha's jaw dropped open. "How dare you!" she said.

Mrs. Braddock didn't flinch a muscle or bat an eyelash. "There's a stagecoach leaving for El Paso the day after tomorrow at ten o'clock in the morning. I will expect you to be on it, or here on this post with your drapes opened, dressed for the day, sober as a judge, and *doing something* for a change. Is that clear!"

Samantha was at the end of her rope. She jumped up from the sofa, balled up her fists, and screeched: *"There's nothing to do here!"*

"There's the post hospital—we can always use a hand there. And there are numerous hungry children in Santa Maria del Pueblo, which is a very interesting little corner of the world, by the way, although I'm sure you haven't noticed because you're the type of snob who can't see anything except other snobs just like yourself."

Samantha stood in the middle of the room. "I am not a snob! How dare you talk to me that way! Who do you think you are!"

"A former snob," Mrs. Braddock said. "But I was able to overcome it and so can you, if you want to, but of course you might prefer to remain a snob all your life—many snobs do, you know. For my part, I prefer the company of the men and women who are fighting for an expanding America here on the frontier, instead of drinking dainty little cups of tea in the drawing rooms of Philadelphia and Boston, discussing the latest fashions, and who did what to whom. To hell with that! I'm a soldier's wife, and proud of it!"

Mrs. Braddock got to her feet and stood erectly, her shoulders squared. Although she was in her fifties, she appeared durable, capable of shooting Apaches with a rifle. She and Samantha looked at each other for a few moments, and then Samantha felt herself unraveling. Her body was wracked with a sob. Mrs. Braddock stepped toward her and wrapped her in her arms.

"Easy now," she said, patting Samantha on the back. "Let it all come out. You'll feel a lot better if you do. We all go through something like this—it's nothing new. You'll survive just as I did, and after a while you'll be quite happy and never dream of going back to Boston again. In years to come you'll look back on this day and wonder what the big fuss was about. You can't be a little girl forever, you know. Once you understand that, you'll be just fine."

The Apache raiding party was gathered at the end of a large clear pool surrounded by rippled black lava and shaded with the leafy branches of ash, buckthorn, willow, and sycamore trees. Horses slurped water noisily as the Apaches filled their canteens.

Coyotero screwed the top back on his canteen. He'd removed his shirt, and wore only his breechclout, moccasin boots, and two bandoliers of ammunition crisscrossing his barrel chest. He glanced up at the position of the sun in the sky, and saw that it was shortly after midday.

Red Feather walked up to him, a stern expression on his face. "I think I know where we are going."

"Fill your canteen," Coyotero replied. "We do not have time to waste with foolish chatter."

"If we continue in the direction we are traveling, we will come to the McIntyre ranch. Is that where you intend to conduct your raid?"

Coyotero looked into his eyes. "Stay out of my way, Medicine Man. I do not have the great reverence for you that others have. You are here only because I have been forced to bring you. The less you speak to me, the better I will like it."

Red Feather stood his ground. "I must speak with you about this, Coyotero. It is a terrible thing you are planning to do, if you are going to raid the McIntyre ranch. The McIntyre people have always been our friends. We have taken their water and grass for many years, even when I and Jacinto were young warriors, even younger than you are right now. We have eaten with them in their house, and they have drunk *titswin* with us in our camp. Ralph McIntyre and Jacinto have cut their arms and mixed their blood together. Jacinto's sons have played with Ralph McIntyre's sons. The mountain spirits would not look kindly upon anyone who would disturb such a friendship."

"Friendship?" asked Coyotero sneeringly. "There can be no friendship between the people and the white eyes. We are at war, and anyone who does not understand that is a fool. If you do not like what we are doing, return to the camp with the women and the old men. We do not need you here."

"No," Red Feather said. "I am not going back. Jacinto asked me to be here, and I shall continue." He turned to the others and held out his arms to them. "Beware of what you are doing, warriors! Do not turn from the noble path of your ancestors. If you kill friends, the mountain spirits will not smile upon you. They will turn their faces from you, unless you stop now."

Coyotero moved toward him belligerently. "You are a ridiculous old man. The people are being crowded out of their land because of the decisions of old men like you. I do not believe you know anything about what the mountain spirits want. I think they want us to fight and kill for what is right. I think they would rather see us die like warriors than live like slaves of the white eyes."

Red Feather wrinkled his brow. "You are not a medicine man. You are just a killer. You are blinded by hatred. Whatever you do will be turned into poison." Red Feather turned to the other warriors again. "Do not listen to this man. I, Red Feather, a medicine man of the people, warn you most solemnly. This man will lead you to your doom. This man will . . ."

With an angry snarl, Coyotero grabbed Red Feather by the throat and pressed his thumbs against his Adam's apple. Red Feather wrapped his fingers around Coyotero's wrists and tried to break loose, but he wasn't strong enough. Coyotero squeezed with all his strength, and Red Feather turned blue. His eyes bulged out of his head and his tongue stuck out. The warriors watched in dismay as Red Feather's life was choked out of him. No one dared defy Coyotero.

Red Feather coughed and gurgled. Then something snapped in his throat and his body went limp. Coyotero let him fall to the ground.

"Let us move on," Coyotero said, striding toward his horse.

5

STONE, LOBO, AND Juanita passed through a thick tangled jungle of boulders, cactuses, trees, and bushes. Occasionally they had to stop so Lobo could scout the area on foot and find out which way would be the easiest to proceed.

They lunched in the shadow of a butte that was wider on top than it was on the bottom, and then continued to work their way through the dense terrain, as cactus needles scratched their skin and tore their clothes.

In midafternoon they climbed to the top of a hill and found themselves looking down into a wide basin that was green, flat, and stunningly beautiful all the way to the horizon. In the middle of the basin were farm buildings and a stream. Herds of cattle and horses grazed in bunches all across the basin.

Lobo pointed down. "That is where we are going to get your horse fixed."

Stone stared in amazement at the bucolic scene below him. It was so completely unexpected. He'd had this experience many times since coming onto the frontier. Without warning the terrain would change into something different and astonishing, like a painting that was the work of a dreamer with an incredible imagination, instead of reality.

"Those white eyes are friends of my father," Lobo said. "I know them well. Their name is McIntyre."

"Why is it your people never bother them?"

"I told you—they are our friends. Come, I will introduce you to them, and they will be your friends too."

Lobo urged his horse down the hill, and Juanita and Stone followed him into the lush green valley.

Lying flat on another hill, Coyotero looked down at the McIntyre ranch. He was especially interested in the horses in the corral. There were nearly forty of them, all fine and sleek. Coyotero had visited the ranch in the past and coveted the horses. Now, soon they would be his.

His eyes roved over the ranch buildings. He knew the McIntyres worked the ranch with about a dozen hired hands, but most of the latter would be out with the cattle. He spotted a young blond woman in a gingham dress near the well. It was Peggy, one of the McIntyre daughters, seventeen years old. Coyotero had always wanted to make her his own.

Coyotero knew that an Apache warrior risked losing his luck in fighting if he raped a female captive, but he didn't believe it. He was a renegade and an apostate among Apaches, and thought the old ways had led the Apaches only to defeat. Now it was time to get rid of the old ways and find new ways. He had contempt for Jacinto and those like him, but had to proceed carefully because most warriors still respected the old ways.

He knew many of the warriors with him were disturbed by the way he'd killed Red Feather, but they were afraid to say anything because they knew he'd kill them too. Coyotero was confident that his warriors would overcome their dismay at the death of Red Feather when they had new horses and new weapons. Coyotero understood the power of greed.

"Coyotero—look!"

It was Black Bear, pointing to the east. Coyotero turned in that direction and saw three riders descending into the valley. He narrowed his eyes and tried to determine who they were, but they were too far away for clear identification.

Coyotero frowned. This was a factor he hadn't considered. Who were these riders? He thought they must be cowboys returning to the ranch. He'd have to wait until they were in the valley before he could proceed with his plan.

The valley was covered with grass nearly as high as a man's hip. Coyotero's plan was to creep unseen with all his warriors through the tall grass to the ranch buildings, and then rise up and attack the McIntyre family. He knew the McIntyres had many rifles and much ammunition, with bridles, wagons, clothes, tools, and all manner of wonderful things. The McIntyres were rich, and soon everything they owned would be his.

"There is a woman among them, I think," said Eagle Claw, squinting his eyes at the three riders approaching the valley. "She is the one in the middle, no?"

Coyotero looked in that direction again and looked at the figure in the middle. They were closer now, and he could see that she was wearing a dress. Then he noticed something familiar about the rider in front. He sat in the saddle similarly to someone he used to know, but who was it?

Then suddenly he recognized the rider. "It is Lobo!" he said.

The others turned in that direction.

"It is so," Black Bear replied, nodding his head. "That surely is Lobo."

"The mountain spirits are smiling on me today," Coyotero said. "They have delivered my enemy Lobo to me. Long have I waited to see him again. This time I will cut his heart out, and no one will dare stop me."

Tom McIntyre was splitting wood behind the main house when he noticed three riders approaching in the distance. At first he thought they were his father's ranch hands and continued hacking at the rounds of wood at his feet. Tom was twenty years old, working with his shirt off, raising the two-and-a-half-pound axe over his head and bringing it down with all his strength, driving it through the length of wood on the ground.

His sister Peggy walked by, carrying a bucket of water toward the back door of the house. Tom placed another chunk of wood on the block and raised the axe. Nearby, in the corral, Bob Smith, one of the ranch hands, tossed a lasso around the neck of a horse, which he was trying to break. Smoke arose from the chimney of the main house; Tom's mother was preparing dinner.

Tom placed another chunk of wood on the block and looked

at the approaching riders again. They were closer now, and he was surprised to realize that they weren't his father's ranch hands. The first was an Apache, the second a woman, and the third a white man.

"Riders!" he called out loudly.

Inside the house, his father, Ralph McIntyre, patriarch of the Double M Ranch, was seated at the desk in his office, doing paperwork. He heard his son's voice and looked out the window behind him.

He saw the three riders, but couldn't recognize who they were. The ranch was in isolated country and visitors were an occasion. Ralph McIntyre took out his old brass spyglass from a shelf and focused it on the three figures approaching down the hill in the distance.

Ralph McIntyre had white hair and long thick sideburns. He was six feet tall and wore red suspenders over his shirt. The figures in the distance became clearer.

"It's Lobo!" he shouted.

In the backyard Tom looked up from the chopping block. He shielded his eyes from the sun and looked at the approaching riders again. Now he could see Lobo on the lead horse. He and Lobo had known each other since they were children. Lobo visited the ranch many times, and Tom had visited Apache encampments. Tom and Lobo had played together, and Lobo had taught him many interesting things about the desert.

Tom leaned his axe against the chopping block and walked toward Lobo and the two people with him. Meanwhile, Ralph McIntyre came out of the house. Father and son stood in the front yard, watching Lobo approach.

They hadn't seen him for a long time. Other Apaches had passed through the area during the past several months, but not Lobo. Relations had been tense lately between Apaches and white people, but the McIntyres thought they'd always be safe because of their long-standing friendship with Jacinto.

The riders came closer. Peggy came out of the house and joined her father and brother. She too knew Lobo and liked him, having played on the desert with her brother and Lobo when she'd been younger. Blond and slender, with pale blue eyes, she wore a white apron over her dress.

Ralph McIntyre, Bob, and Peggy turned their attention to

the two riders with Lobo: a young Mexican woman with black hair, and a tall husky American wearing a wide-brimmed hat low over his eyes, his shirt torn and covered with dried blood. It was a strange combination appearing in their front yard suddenly out of the vast expanses of desert.

Lobo climbed down from his horse and shook hands American-style with Ralph McIntyre and Bob. Then he bowed and murmured a polite greeting to Peggy. Finally he introduced Juanita and John Stone to the McIntyres.

Ralph McIntyre studied Stone as they shook hands. "You look like you've been run over by a herd of cattle."

"I had a difference of opinion with another gentleman, you might say."

"Looks like he damn near killed you." Ralph McIntyre turned to Lobo. "Where you headed?"

"Tucson, but John Stone's horse needs a shoe. Think you can fix us up?"

"There's shoes in the barn—help yourself. Dinner'll be served in about another hour. How's your father?"

"I have not seen him for a long time."

"Why not?"

Lobo turned away, to lead the horses to the barn and avoid Ralph McIntyre's questions. Stone went with him, leaving Juanita standing uncertainly in the yard. Peggy took her hand. "C'mon into the house. You can get cleaned up."

Peggy led Juanita to the house, and Tom looked at Juanita's shapely figure.

"Wonder why Lobo ain't seen his father for a while?" Ralph McIntyre said, rubbing his stubbled chin with the tips of his fingers. "Something must've happened. Hope it wasn't serious."

The Apache raiding party crawled through the high grass, heading toward the McIntyre ranch. They'd seen Lobo arrive with the two strangers and saw Lobo and the white eyes take their horses to the barn. A total of eight people were in the vicinity, counting the women and the newcomers, and Coyotero had twenty-four warriors. He expected a fast easy fight, and then plenty of loot.

Coyotero was overjoyed to have Lobo nearby, because he

considered Lobo his mortal enemy. All his life, even when he was a little boy, he'd hated Lobo because Lobo was the son of Jacinto, and one day Lobo could be expected to become chief of the tribe.

Coyotero thought he was a better man than Lobo, and he deserved to be chief because of his fighting skill and intelligence. He considered Lobo weak-minded because Lobo had never been especially eager to go to war. Lobo liked to sit alone on the desert in the middle of the night and look at the stars, and had been overly polite to the old fools who called themselves medicine men, fools like Red Feather. Worst of all, everybody liked Lobo, while everybody feared Coyotero.

Coyotero thought his ascension to chief of the tribe would be assured if he killed Lobo, and now Lobo was within his grasp. No one would stop him from killing Lobo this time.

Before entering the tall grass, he'd given orders to his warriors. When they attacked, they were to kill everybody except Lobo and Peggy. Coyotero wanted the pleasure of killing Lobo himself, and Peggy would become his slave. Coyotero smiled as he crawled silently through the grass. *This is my lucky day.*

While the food cooked, Juanita helped Peggy set the long table in the dining room.

"Why are you going to Tucson?" Peggy asked, placing a plate at the head of the table, where her father customarily sat.

"*Bandidos* are after us," Juanita said. "John Stone killed Rodrigo, their leader, in a knife fight."

"What did they fight about?"

"Me."

"Really?"

Juanita described the events leading to the fight, while down the hall Ralph McIntyre listened in his office. He knew who Rodrigo was and had suspected him and his men of rustling some of the Double M cattle over the years, but Rodrigo never rustled that much, and McIntyre never had been able to catch him.

"After Stone kill Rodrigo with his knife," Juanita continued, "Rodrigo's men started shooting. Stone would have been killed, but the Indian saved his life. Then all three of us leave pronto."

"How did Stone know Lobo?" Peggy asked.

"I do not think they ever saw each other until that night."

Peggy wasn't surprised by the story, because it was similar to other stories she'd heard throughout her life. People always were getting shot and knifed in nearby towns, Apaches always were massacring ranchers and settlers, bandits stole everything that wasn't nailed down, and the cavalry chased the Apaches all over the desert, usually never finding them.

"John Stone is one tough hombre," Juanita said as she placed a fork beside a plate. "I never thought the man lived who could kill Rodrigo, but John Stone did it. I would not be standing here right now if it was not for John Stone."

The Apaches crawled closer to the ranch. Black Bear and Eagle Claw, the two former disciples of Red Feather, were side by side ten feet behind Coyotero, and they continually looked at each other in a troubled way, because they'd weren't happy about Coyotero's murder of Red Feather.

Black Bear and Eagle Claw wanted horses and guns, but they were disturbed by the way Coyotero had choked Red Feather to death. Red Feather had been a respected medicine man with supernatural powers. He'd cured the sick and predicted the future, and was believed to be in communion with the mountain spirits.

Black Bear and Eagle Claw had been taken by surprise when Coyotero grabbed Red Feather by the throat. They'd wanted to intervene, but were afraid of Coyotero, and Red Feather had been dead before they'd made up their minds about what to do.

It was bad luck to kill a medicine man. Coyotero flaunted Apache traditions whenever he felt like it, but Yusn never punished him. Coyotero grew stronger and more powerful all the time. His raids were always successful, and raiding was an essential component of Apache economic life. The mountain spirits approved of what Coyotero did, since they gave him so much success, but Coyotero had choked Red Feather to death, and Red Feather had been a great medicine man.

A horse whinnied in the distance, and the Apaches thought of the horses in the corral. Each had visited the McIntyre ranch in the past and admired the many fine horses. Soon they'd own the horses, and horses were wealth to the Apaches. They'd have new weapons too, and a good weapon could be the difference between life and death.

Black Bear and Eagle Claw were afraid, and so were several of the other Apaches in the raiding party. They weren't afraid of dying because they were warriors to the core and death was their constant companion. Their fear was of the unknown world ruled by the spirits, who might be offended by the murder of Red Feather.

None of the warriors dared stand up to Coyotero, and it would be cowardly to turn back from a raid after having made preparations for it. They all wanted horses and guns, and they all hated the white eyes. They agreed with Coyotero that the white eyes must be fought wherever they were found, and no peace was possible with them. They even believed that the McIntyres were fair game, for the McIntyres were white eyes, and the white eyes were crushing life out of the Apache people.

They crept onward through the peaceful afternoon, while ahead of them, in the ranch house, the McIntyre family and their guests were sitting down to dinner.

The table was covered with pots and serving dishes, and delicious aromas filled the air as Ralph McIntyre said grace, his big gnarled red hands clasped together. "Lord," he said, "we thank You for the bounty of this table, for we know all good things come from You. Please bless this food and drink, and we hope it will give us the strength to do Your will. Amen. Dig in, folks."

Martha McIntyre, a stout woman who wore eyeglasses, removed the covers from the pots and serving dishes, which were passed around the table. The main course was a huge roast beef swimming in gravy, garnished with potatoes and carrots. A loaf of freshly baked bread sat on a board in the middle of the table, beside a tub of cow butter.

Stone was wearing a clean shirt that Ralph McIntyre had given him. It had two pockets with buttoned flaps and was made of dark green canvas.

"Where are you from, Mr. Stone?" Ralph McIntyre asked, slicing into his meat.

"South Carolina—not far from Columbia. How about you?"

"I was born in Arkansas, but my daddy came here when I was small. He started this ranch, and I'm doing my best to keep it going."

"It's a beautiful spread. I'd like to have something like it for myself someday."

"There's a lot of land out here. You'll need money to get started, but that's usually not too hard to get. Just work for a while and save it up. Lots of men began that way. I'd offer you a job here, but I understand you're anxious to get to Tucson. Too bad, because I could always use a good man."

"If you've been in this country all your life," Stone said, "I imagine you've seen quite a bit of it."

"I've done my share of traveling," McIntyre agreed.

Stone took out the picture of Marie and passed it over the table to him. "Ever see this woman?"

Ralph McIntyre held the picture in front of him and squinted his eyes, staring at it for several seconds. "She looks familiar," he said.

Stone was surprised. People generally said they didn't recognize her, and he'd been getting used to it. "You think you've seen her?" he asked.

Ralph McIntyre continued to look at the picture. "I can't say for sure, but I think I have. About two years ago I was in Texas, talking with some ranchers there, and if my memory is right, this woman was married to one of them ranchers."

"Are you sure this is that woman?"

McIntyre looked down at the picture. "I wouldn't want to bet my life on it, but they sure look the same." He raised the picture closer to his eyes. "Yep, I do believe it's her."

"Do you remember her name, by any chance?"

" 'Fraid not. There were so many people there, and I didn't do any business with her husband, as I recall."

"What was her husband like?"

"Much older than her, if my recollection is right, a real gentleman, and she was quite a lady. If I'm not mistaken, she had an accent pretty much like yours."

"What part of Texas was it?"

"San Antone." Ralph McIntyre handed the picture back. Who is she?"

"I was supposed to marry her, but when I came home from the war she was gone. I've been looking for her ever since, and this is the first time in four years that anybody's said he's seen her."

"I want to make it clear to you," Ralph McIntyre replied, "that I wouldn't stake my life on what I've just told you, but I think it's the same woman. Somehow she stayed in my mind. She was a real good-looker, and polite as can be, a real lady."

Stone put the picture back into his pocket. Was Marie in San Antone? If so, he was headed in the wrong direction. Tucson was west, and San Antone east. But he couldn't go east now, because the Mexican bandits were looking for him. He'd have to continue to Tucson and then catch a stage coming back via another route, probably a northerly one, maybe to Santa Fe. From Santa Fe he could continue east toward Texas. Possibly, in another two or three weeks, a month at the most, he could be in San Antone.

Stone tried to be calm as he ate his meal. Vaguely he was aware of Lobo and Ralph McIntyre talking about Jacinto and the Apaches in the area, but his mind was on Marie, possibly so close to him now. If she was the woman Mr. McIntyre was talking about, why had she got married to that old man? Who was he and where did she meet him? Marie always had good manners, and could be described as a real lady. It sounded like her, but what was she doing in San Antone?

Maybe it wasn't her. Stone had been led astray once before. Someone had told him that Marie was working in a certain saloon, and when he got there, the woman behind the bar looked completely different. The person who'd told him had lied on purpose because he'd wanted Stone to buy him a drink.

But Ralph McIntyre was a different kind of man. He didn't have any tricks up his sleeve. Stone felt happy. He couldn't wait to reach Tucson so he could begin traveling east back to Texas again.

The windows were open and a cool breeze blew through the dining room. Out in the desert a bird sang a lilting song. Juanita took a second helping of meat, because she was so hungry. She looked like a gypsy with her golden earrings flashing in the afternoon light. She was the exact opposite of Peggy McIntyre, who was light-skinned, dainty, and well groomed, but Peggy hadn't been living on the desert like an Apache for the past two days.

Mrs. McIntyre asked Lobo about his mother's health, and a scowl came over Lobo's face. "I have not seen her for a long time," he said.

The expression on his face suggested he didn't want to talk about it more, and Mrs. McIntyre took the hint, turning her attention to Juanita. "Are you from Santa Maria del Pueblo?" she asked.

"All my life," Juanita replied, "but it has not been much of a life, I am sorry to say."

"What did you do there?"

"I was a singer at La Rosita. Do you know La Rosita?"

"I don't believe so," Mrs. McIntyre said pleasantly.

Juanita pointed to John Stone. "La Rosita is where he killed my boyfriend."

There was a sudden lull in conversation. Everyone looked at Stone, who felt embarrassed. "Self-defense," he said. "The man pulled a knife on me." He turned to Ralph McIntyre, to change the topic of conversation. "How many head of cattle do you have?"

Suddenly there was an earsplittting war whoop, and an Apache Indian jumped through the window, somersaulting through the air and landing on his feet on the floor beside the table, war paint all over his face, holding a rifle in his hand. The door burst open and several Apaches charged into the dining room. Simultaneously another Apache dived through the other window.

John Stone jumped to his feet and drew both of his guns, opening fire. More Apaches poured into the room, triggering rifles and pistols, slashing with knives. The room filled with screams and gunsmoke and it was difficult to see what was going on.

At the far end of the table, Bob Smith, the hired hand, reached for his six-gun. Coyotero turned toward him and pulled the trigger of his rifle. The bullet struck Smith in the chest. He went sprawling backward, crashing into the wall.

Tom McIntyre reached for his gun too. One of the Apache warriors, Many Horses, let fly an arrow, which struck the young man in the chest. He staggered backward, trying to pull the arrow out of his chest, and then another Apache, Fast As a Fox, jumped forward and split his head open with a hatchet.

The women screamed in horror, jumping up, their fists near their mouths as Bob Smith and Tom McIntyre bled onto the floor. Martha McIntyre rushed toward her son and bent over him, her face wrenched in shock. Black Bear whacked her over the head with a hatchet, and she collapsed on top of her son.

Ralph McIntyre wore no weapon. In the initial moments of the attack, he stood at the head of the table and picked up his steak knife, preparing to defend himself, but Tacho, one of the Apaches, ran him through the chest with his long lance. He fell to his knees, and Tacho pulled the lance out. Ralph McIntyre fell forward, and was dead before he hit the floor.

Peggy McIntyre saw her father fall, and fainted dead away. Coyotero drew his long knife and prepared to stab Juanita when she screeched and dived on him, fighting for her life. She was strong, but no match for Coyotero. He pinned her wrists to the wall and looked into her eyes. Something he saw there made him pause. "Save this one for me too!" he said to his men.

He turned around. The room was still full of smoke. In the far corner, Lobo stood in front of John Stone, and a phalanx of Apaches surrounded Lobo, pointing their rifles, pistols, and lances at him. Stone's pistols were in his hands, ready to fire again. Blood was everywhere. Bodies lay all over the floor.

Lobo held a pistol in his right hand, and a thin trail of smoke arose from its barrel. His body was tense and poised to fight, as he looked around the room. "So Coyotero is now a killer of women," he said in a low deadly voice.

Coyotero sneered. "It is Lobo, friend of the white eyes. I am so happy to see you again, so that I can kill you."

"What is the meaning of this?" Lobo asked. "These people have always been our friends."

"Not anymore," Coyotero replied. "Who is that white eyes behind you, who you are trying to protect?"

"He is my blood brother. If you kill him, you must kill me first."

"It will be as you say," Coyotero told him. "I will kill you first, and then I will kill him."

Coyotero and Lobo were hollering at each other in their language, and Stone couldn't understand what they were saying, but knew he was in trouble. Dead bodies were all over the floor. He held both his Colts in his hands, and was ready for anything.

"Coward!" Lobo shouted at Coyotero. "You attack people who have always been our friends! You have no honor! You are nothing but a killer of women!"

"You are the little brown pet of the white eyes!" Coyotero replied with a sneer. "They treat you like a dog, and you lick their hands! You are a traitor to your people! You should be killed!"

"Kill me then, if you dare! You talk like a warrior, but you are only good for killing women!"

"I would have killed you once, if your father hadn't stopped me! The worms would be eating your guts right now, if it weren't for your father!"

"Why don't you try again, and see what happens to you?"

Coyotero stared at Lobo malevolently, hating him with every fiber of his being. "Be careful of what you say," he replied. "This time you don't have your father to save you."

"No one is here to save you either. Last time you were lucky. Are you a warrior who only fights women, or are you a warrior who dares to fight a real man?"

Coyotero laughed. "Who is the real man supposed to be? Surely not you, who hides behind his father."

"My father isn't here now." Lobo beckoned with his finger. "Come on—just you and me together. Guns, knives, bare hands, any way you like. What are you afraid of?"

"I am not afraid of you, that is for sure."

"If you are not afraid of me, why don't you fight me?" Lobo looked at the other warriors, all of whom he knew. "How can you follow a man who is afraid to fight? You have all heard me challenge him, and what does he say? Only words. If he were a real warrior, he would accept my challenge, go outside with me, and prove who is the best fighter."

The warriors looked at Coyotero, to hear his reply, and he felt their eyes burning into him. There was no way he could ignore the challenge. "I have long waited for this day," he said. "If you want to die, I will be happy to oblige you."

Black Bear turned to him. "Coyotero, we don't have time for this. The ranch hands may arrive at any moment, and the bluecoats are on the desert. Let us do what we came here to do and get out of here. If you want to fight Lobo, you can do it someplace else."

"It will not take long to kill Lobo," Coyotero said. "If the ranch hands come, we will kill them too, and the bluecoats are far away. Let us go outside. This time no one will stop me from killing Lobo."

Nolga aimed his pistol at John Stone. "Drop your guns."

Stone hesitated.

Lobo said to him: "Do as he tells you. I will get us out of this."

Stone didn't want to disarm himself, but if he didn't, they'd kill him. His Colts went crashing to the floor, and Eagle Claw eagerly picked them up.

Coyotero turned to Lobo. "Outside! Move!" Coyotero pointed at the door with his rifle. "Bring the women," he said to his warriors.

Tacho prodded Juanita with his rifle, and she stepped toward the door. She didn't know what was going on. Her lips trembled as she recited Hail Marys and Our Fathers one after the other. Two warriors picked up the still unconscious Peggy and carried her outside.

The sun shone brightly on the yard in front of the house, as the Apaches and their prisoners emerged from the front door. The barrel of Nolga's rifle touched the small of Stone's back as he stepped onto the ground.

"What's going to happen now?" Stone asked Lobo, who was in front of him.

"I am going to fight Coyotero. When I beat him, we all go free."

Stone was about to ask: *What if you don't beat him*? but decided there was no point in planting the seed of defeat in his mind.

They walked into the front yard on the other side of the hitching posts. Black Bear approached Coyotero, whose facial expression was cold and determined.

"This is great foolishness," Black Bear protested. "We should take what we want and get out of here as soon as possible. If you wish to fight Lobo, you can fight him back at the camp."

"The time to fight him is now," Coyotero said with finality.

Black Bear moved away from Coyotero. Everyone gathered on the open ground between the house and barn. Coyotero faced the hills and waved his hand in the air. A few moments later Apache warriors appeared on the crest of the hill, herding horses toward the ranch house. Stone guessed these were the horses the Apaches had ridden to the ranch. They'd left them in the hills while Coyotero and the others had crept up on the main building.

The sound of hoofbeats came from the opposite direction. Everyone turned and saw a white man, evidently one of the McIntyre ranch hands, walking toward them, blood streaming from a wound on his scalp, and behind him was a mounted Apache carrying a rifle.

"Look what I found!" the Apache said.

"We will take care of him when we are finished here," Coyotero said. Then Coyotero turned to Lobo. "This is where you will die. How do you want it?"

"It is up to you," Lobo said.

"How about knives, like last time?"

Lobo unbuttoned his cavalry shirt, as Coyotero drew his knife out of its sheath. The Apaches and their captives formed a wide circle in the yard between the barn and the ranch house. Lobo and Coyotero were in the middle of the circle, and Stone couldn't help noticing the contrast between the two.

Lobo was calm, almost casual, whereas Coyotero was a flame of hatred. Lobo's naked upper body was smoothly muscled, with a few nicks and cuts. He was taller and leaner than Coyotero, and several years younger. He pulled out his knife, and a sunbeam rolled along the blade.

Coyotero wore only his breechclout and moccasin boots. Muscles were knotted and bunched all over his thick body. His face was a mask of hatred. He held his knife in his fist with the blade pointed straight up in the air.

"I am waiting," he said.

Lobo turned and faced him, holding his knife in his fist also. "I am ready. Let us begin."

Coyotero went into a crouch, bending his knees, and appeared tense as the string of a bow pulled taut to fire an arrow.

Lobo was relaxed and almost casual, and sauntered to the side within the circle. Coyotero followed him on the balls of his feet, ready to spring. To Stone's eyes, Coyotero looked far deadlier than Lobo. Stone was struck with the sinking feeling that Lobo was going to lose, and if he lost, Stone would be killed.

No one else said anything as Coyotero circled Lobo and Lobo strolled around the circle, his head cocked to one side, holding his knife in his fingertips. Coyotero feinted, and Lobo didn't respond. That concerned Stone, because if it hadn't been a feint, Lobo would've been cut. It seemed to Stone that Lobo wasn't really keyed up enough for the fight. He appeared much too calm and cool, as if he didn't care about what was going on.

Coyotero feinted again, and again Lobo didn't make a move to defend himself. Coyotero's legs were spread far apart and his knees were bent, reminding Stone of a crab. He flicked the point of his blade back and forth, and his face was expressionless.

Stone noticed the solemn expression on the faces of the Apaches. Juanita watched the fight also, and Stone knew what she was thinking. She was hoping Lobo would win, because otherwise she'd be killed, and her manner of dying probably wouldn't be pleasant.

Stone looked at Peggy, not far from Juanita. Peggy was conscious, but her face was like snow and she appeared to be in a trance. In a matter of seconds her parents and brother had been killed, and something had snapped in her mind.

Coyotero continued to circle Lobo, changing direction back and forth, and Lobo watched him calmly, holding his knife in front of him, his skin like bronze in the sunlight. Suddenly Coyotero lunged forward, streaking the point of his blade toward Lobo's midsection. Lobo darted to the side and made a sudden movement with his knife. Coyotero found himself facing his warriors, and Lobo was several feet away. When Coyotero turned toward Lobo again, Stone could see a deep gash on Coyotero's left pectoral muscle.

First blood, Stone thought.

Coyotero's face showed no recognition that he'd been wounded as he closed in on Lobo again, and Lobo showed no exultation. The stalking continued as before. Coyotero continued to advance, trying to get closer to Lobo, and Lobo danced out of reach easily. Coyotero clearly was the pursuer, forcing the fight, and Lobo evidently wanted to counter off Coyotero's attacks.

"Why do you run away from me?" Coyotero asked mockingly. "Are you afraid?"

"Come closer," Lobo replied. "There's something I want to give you."

They stalked each other in the center of the circle, and then in a movement so fast it was a blur, Coyotero pounced again, slashing at Lobo's throat, but Lobo wasn't there, and when Coyotero turned around to face Lobo again, Coyotero had a cut on his left shoulder. Blood dribbled down his arm like a thin red ribbon. Lobo had struck, and no one had seen him do it.

Stone watched carefully, recalling his own knife fight at La Rosita two days ago. He could see now more clearly than ever the importance of speed. *If I ever get out of this*, he said to himself, *I've got to practice speed*.

Coyotero jumped again, and Lobo dodged to the side, but this time Coyotero anticipated his move and followed him, slashing wildly with his knife. The point of his knife pierced Lobo's right cheek and penetrated to the bone, cutting down to the chin. Lobo stepped backward and spun away as blood sprayed through the air. Coyotero charged, driving his knife toward Lobo's kidney, and Lobo grabbed Coyotero's wrist, stopping it in midair, while driving his own blade toward Coyotero's guts.

Coyotero's hand clamped onto Lobo's wrist, and they were locked together tightly, only inches apart, blood oozing out of the slash on Lobo's face and the two cuts on Coyotero's body. They heaved and pushed each other, gritting their teeth, each trying to force his blade into the skin of his opponent, when suddenly Lobo dropped to his back on the ground and arched violently, pushing his foot into Coyotero's belly and tossing Coyotero behind him.

Coyotero went flying through the air and landed on his face in the dust, while meanwhile, behind him, Lobo jumped to his feet and charged. Coyotero arose and Lobo ripped his knife across Coyotero's back, leaving a wide deep cut from

Coyotero's right shoulder to the left side of his waist.

Coyotero snarled like an animal and jumped around to face Lobo, while Lobo bounced backward out of reach. Coyotero advanced, and Lobo moved to the side again. Lobo's cheek was covered with blood, while Coyotero bled copiously from his three wounds. The ground beneath them was flecked with blood, and blood covered their knives.

Fascinated, Stone watched the fight. Now it was clear to him what Lobo's strategy was. Lobo evidently didn't want to match strength with Coyotero. He was trying to defeat Coyotero with maneuverability.

Coyotero and Lobo circled each other. Black Bear scanned the horizon nervously, worrying about armed ranch hands and the bluecoats. He wished the fight would end soon. Every passing moment increased the danger to all of them.

Coyotero grunted and swooped toward Lobo, and Lobo jumped out of the way, but in a sudden move, Coyotero dived toward Lobo's feet, slashed out with his knife, tumbled over and landed on his feet again, advancing murderously toward Lobo, whose right boot and calf muscle were neatly severed. Blood poured down Lobo's ankle and filled his boot as he limped away from Coyotero.

Now Stone understood Coyotero's counter-strategy. Coyotero realized he had to slow Lobo down, and one way to do it was to cripple him.

Stone could see that Lobo was slowed seriously. Lobo no longer had any spring in his movements. He wouldn't be able to get away from Coyotero so easily now, but his face showed no awareness of his predicament. He still seemed calm and unconcerned. Coyotero didn't acknowledge that he'd just given himself an advantage.

Coyotero charged Lobo again, and Lobo tried to get out of the way, but this time wasn't fast enough. Coyotero rammed his knife toward Lobo's belly, and Lobo grabbed Coyotero's wrist, stopping its forward movement while making a threatening gesture with his own knife toward Coyotero's throat. Coyotero raised his free hand to stop the threat, but it was only a feint. In a quick move, Lobo brought his knife down and took a swipe at Coyotero's belly.

Coyotero sucked wind and pulled back. There was a two-inch

gash on Coyotero's stomach. Coyotero showed no consciousness of the pain. He circled Lobo as before, and Lobo limped away from him. Coyotero feinted to his left, feinted to his right, let out a cry, and rushed Lobo again, tossing his knife from his left hand to his right hand, and Lobo made a quick motion with his arm. There was a *clink* sound and Coyotero's knife flew straight up into the air. Coyotero was unarmed, and Lobo leaned forward, touching the tip of his blade to Coyotero's throat, pressing firmly, and the blade entered Coyotero's throat an eighth of an inch.

"Don't move," Lobo said.

Coyotero froze, as blood dripped out of the hole Lobo's knife had made.

"Hear me carefully," Lobo said. "We fought once before, and you nearly killed me, but you stopped. Now we fight again, and I can kill you, but I'm going to stop. You gave me my life back, and now I shall give you your life back. We're even, a life for a life, but we're not finished. I propose that we fight again, tomorrow at noon, and in that fight neither of us will give the other his life back. That fight will be to the death."

"It will be as you say," Coyotero said stiffly, blood trickling down his throat.

"Furthermore," Lobo continued, "you and your warriors must agree on your honor not to harm my blood brother here, the Mexican woman, or Peggy McIntyre as long as I am alive. And you must return the weapons you took from my blood brother and me."

"It is agreed," Coyotero said. "You have my word as a warrior on all the points that you mentioned, and the winner of the fight tomorrow can do anything he wants with the prisoners."

"It will be as you say," Lobo told him.

Lobo pulled his knife out of Coyotero's throat and took a step backward, wiping his knife against his pant leg, and pushing it into its sheath on his belt. Coyotero bent over and picked up his own knife, wiping it on his thigh. Then he looked up at his men. If he was ashamed of losing the fight, he didn't show it.

"Take the horses out of the corral," he told them. "Load a wagon with booty. Set fire to the buildings." He pointed at the captured ranch hand, whose name was Morgan. "You know what to do with him."

"Wait a minute," Lobo said. "You promised not to harm any of these people."

"I promised not to harm your blood brother, the Mexican woman, or Peggy McIntyre. You didn't say anything about the ranch hand. I will honor our agreement as you stated it. Take care that you honor your part."

Stone spoke: "I want my guns."

Lobo turned to Eagle Claw. "Give him his guns."

Eagle Claw looked at Coyotero for guidance, and Coyotero scrutinized Stone carefully. Then Coyotero said: "Give the white eyes his guns. Tomorrow, after I kill Lobo, I will kill the white eyes and give you the guns back."

Eagle Claw walked toward Stone and held out the guns. Stone took them and felt better immediately.

The circle broke apart as the warriors followed Coyotero's orders. Some ran to the barn, others to the corral, and a third group charged toward the main ranch house. Four Apaches grabbed Morgan by his arms and legs and carried him off as he screamed and fought to break loose.

The exchanges between Lobo and Coyotero had been in the Apache language, and Stone didn't understand a word. "What's going on?" he said to Lobo.

Lobo explained everything. Juanita walked toward them, her arm around Peggy's shoulders. Peggy still appeared to be in shock.

"She cannot talk," Juanita said, looking sideways at Peggy. "I think she has gone loco in the coco."

Stone stood in front of Peggy and looked into her eyes. They were glassy and staring. "Are you all right?" Stone asked her.

The features of her pretty face sagged, and lines existed where none had been before. She had a vacuous expression, gazing off into space. Her lips didn't move.

"She's lost her mind," Stone said.

"That's what I told you," Juanita replied.

Stone turned to Lobo. "That was some fight."

"I made mistakes," Lobo said.

"Where are we going now?"

"You will meet my father," Lobo said. "He is a great chief and a very wise man. Tomorrow I will fight Coyotero again. If I kill him, all of you can leave. If he kills me, you will not leave. He probably will kill you, and the women will be his slaves."

"Personally," Stone said. "I think you should've killed him while you had the chance."

"I would rather do it this way."

"What about the women?"

"I would rather do it this way."

Stone looked at Lobo and realized he didn't know him at all. Meanwhile, Apaches harnessed horses to a wagon and backed it up to the front door of the main ranch house, where they loaded it with the possessions of the McIntyre family. They chattered excitedly and sang victory songs. Other Apaches herded the horses out of the corral.

Peggy stared at the horizon mindlessly. Stone rolled a cigarette and passed the tobacco to Lobo, who sat on the ground while Juanita bandaged his leg with a length of material torn from her petticoat. Lobo was in a bad mood, and the side of his face was caked with blood.

"I should not have let him cut my leg," he said bitterly. "I should have been ready for him. He will not do it again."

The wagon was filled with rifles, ammunition, blankets, clothing, food, harnesses, saddles, and trinkets. Another wagon was rolled into the open area between the ranch houses and the barn. The four Indians holding Morgan wrestled him to the ground, turned him upside down, and tied him up to a wagon wheel as he hollered and struggled to break loose.

"What're they going to do with him?" Stone asked Lobo.

"He is going to die," Lobo replied.

Juanita looked at Lobo. "You Apaches are savages!"

"Mexicans have done far worse to us. There was a time when your dirty government offered one hundred dollars for the scalp of every Apache man, fifty dollars for every woman, and twenty-five dollars for every child."

The Apaches placed some dry grass, twigs, and sticks of wood underneath Morgan's head, and Morgan shrieked horribly. Peggy didn't react; she continued to stare at the horizon. Juanita jammed her fingers in her ears. Stone thumbed fresh cartridges into his Colts as his cigarette dangled out of the corner of his mouth.

Lobo walked to Peggy and placed his arm around her shoulders. "I am very sorry about what happened to your family," he said softly. "I will help you as much as I can."

She didn't respond. Lobo removed his arm from her shoulders and looked at Stone, who dropped his Colts into their holsters. The screams of Morgan were unnerving him. He glanced toward him, and the hapless ranch hand writhed upside down on the wagon wheel, as the Apaches set fire to the dry grass and twigs underneath his head.

Coyotero marched out of the house. "Bring the horses around!"

The fire caught underneath Morgan's head, and he screamed desperately, blubbering, praying to God, a flood of mad gibberish bursting out of his mouth. His hair began to burn, and the skin on his head turned red. He kicked and struggled against the ropes, to no avail. Stone looked away and swallowed hard.

Saddled horses were brought into the courtyard, and an Apache led one to Stone, who climbed onto it. Lobo helped Peggy onto a horse. Apaches ran about with torches, setting fire to the house, barn, and outbuildings.

Morgan's screams became whimpers, and then he stopped altogether. Stone turned to him out of morbid curiosity, and Morgan's head had become a dark purple color nearly submerged completely in the fire blazing beneath him. A terrible stench filled the air.

"Move out!" Coyotero shouted.

The Apache in the wagon whipped the team of horses, and they pulled their heavy load of stolen goods away from the burning buildings. Stone, Lobo, and the others followed the wagon, and Coyotero galloped forward to a position in front of the wagon, leading the way back to the desert.

The Apache warriors yipped and yelled victoriously, brandishing their new rifles, grinning happily. Stone turned around in his saddle and looked back at the ranch buildings engulfed in flames, sending columns of black smoke rising into the sky.

6

LIEUTENANT LOWELL SAT in his saddle and gazed through his spyglass at the smoke in the distance. Sergeant McFeeley was at his side, and the patrol of troopers was behind them, drinking from their canteens, grateful for the opportunity to take a break.

Lieutenant Lowell lowered his spyglass. "What do you make of it?" he asked Tim Connors, his chief of scouts.

"Apaches," Connors replied.

Lieutenant Lowell opened his map case to see what was in the direction of the smoke.

"The McIntyre ranch is all that's over there," Connors said.

"I thought the Apaches didn't bother them."

"Don't know what else it could be."

Lieutenant Lowell spread out his map to be sure, and the McIntyre ranch was in the direction of the smoke. The only thing to do was break off his search for John Stone and investigate the smoke.

"How far away would you say the ranch is?" Lieutenant Lowell asked.

"A few hours if we don't dawdle."

"We'll move out right now. Take the point, Mr. Connors."

Connors saluted and rode off with his two Apache scouts, heading toward the smoke in the distance. Lieutenant Lowell nudged his horse and followed them. The rest of the patrol came after him, the guidon fluttering in the breeze.

Lieutenant Lowell wasn't particularly surprised by the possibility of an attack on the McIntyre ranch. He had no reason to believe they'd honor special arrangements with white people. The officers at the post often had speculated that someday the Apaches would turn on the McIntyres, and Lieutenant Lowell knew for a fact that Colonel Braddock had warned Ralph McIntyre personally about the dangers of ranching in the midst of Apaches, but Ralph McIntyre believed Jacinto would protect him.

Maybe it's just a grass fire, he thought as he led the patrol toward the smoke in the distance. *Maybe the McIntyres are all right*.

In a rocky gulch filled with prickly pear cactus, Antonio looked at the smoke rising beyond the mountains. He'd lived on or near the desert long enough to know what it meant: Apaches had set something on fire.

Miguel stood beside him, also watching the smoke disappear into the atmosphere. "There is a big ranchero out that way," he said. "Maybe that is what's burning."

"I think we have been here long enough," Antonio replied. "We should start moving again."

"In what direction?" Miguel asked.

"Tucson."

Miguel opened his mouth to argue, but thought he'd better keep quiet. He didn't want to risk making Antonio mad. Antonio had a vicious temper, especially when he was hot and cranky.

Antonio lifted his canteen to his lips and took a gulp. He wanted to drink more, but only had an inch or two of water left at the bottom of his canteen.

"We need to find water," Antonio said. "Are there any water holes around here?"

"There is one two hours away, but we must be careful. Apaches attack travelers at water holes."

"Lead us there," Antonio told him. "Water is our main concern right now. You will scout the water hole carefully before we go in."

Miguel adjusted his gunbelt around his waist and walked toward his horse, tightening the cinch straps, climbing into the saddle.

He rode out of the gulch and headed toward the water hole. Antonio and the others mounted up behind him, and he could hear them following.

Miguel's shirt was plastered to his body with sweat. All he wanted was a cool drink and a hot woman. He peered suspiciously around him, knowing Apaches could be anywhere. They could blend in with the desert and you wouldn't know they were there until you were right on top of them.

He didn't like the signs. He'd seen three Apaches earlier in the day, and now they'd set something on fire. Apaches were on the warpath, and he was riding directly through their country.

He felt discouraged, because he didn't dare stand up to Antonio, and if Antonio didn't kill him, the Apaches might. *Maybe I should have listened to my grandmother*, he said to himself sadly. *Maybe I should have become a priest.*

Fort Kimball was a few hundred yards from Santa Maria del Pueblo, and Samantha walked toward the town, hoping she'd find something interesting there. She'd visited Santa Maria del Pueblo a few times before, and thought it a filthy little place with no redeeming qualities whatever, but maybe it'd be different this time.

She wore a high-necked blouse and a long skirt with comfortable high-topped boots and a straw hat with a wide flat brim to keep the sun out of her eyes.

Mrs. Braddock had advised her to take a closer look at the town, and that's what she intended to do. She didn't expect much to come of it, but was willing to give it a try. Mrs. Braddock didn't accompany her because she had duties of her own to attend to.

Samantha still was shaken by the events of the day. Her argument with Josh, the liquor, and the tongue-lashing from Mrs. Braddock all combined to make her feel disoriented. Mrs. Braddock had been harsh at first, but then became tender, comforting and encouraging, sort of like a mother. The hug Mrs. Braddock gave her had felt good, but Samantha still didn't think she could be happy in this godforsaken desert community. *I belong in a place like Boston.*

She didn't think she could ever be like Mrs. Braddock, a strong woman who accepted the harsh challenges of military life and overcame them. Samantha didn't see the point of overcoming those challenges. She wanted to enjoy life. Fort Kimball didn't have anything that she wanted except Josh, and she wasn't even sure about him anymore.

The Josh she lived with now was much different from the young officer she'd fallen in love with in Boston. This Josh usually was tired and dirty, and seemed to enjoy being with his soldiers more than her. He was so concerned with his silly old career, and that was no fun for her.

A divorce would be difficult and embarrassing, and there was something about Josh that was extremely appealing. He wasn't the easiest person in the world to get along with, and he didn't give her enough of his time, but they'd only been married a little over a year and she wasn't ready to give up on him yet. Maybe Mrs. Braddock was right, and she could adjust to being the wife of an Army officer.

She found herself on the outskirts of Santa Maria del Pueblo: squat adobe houses scattered about, a few scraggly trees, half-naked Mexican children running around, and a few wagons coming and going, spewing clouds of dust behind them.

She continued toward the center of town, and the adobe houses were closer together, sometimes sharing common walls. Horses were tied to hitching posts in front of stores and saloons, and Mexican and American men and women walked the sidewalks, shopping or otherwise going about their business. Groups of men smoking cigarettes sat on benches in front of the stores, and she was aware that their eyes were on her as she passed.

She came to the central square of the town, and saw the big old church, which she thought crude and grotesque compared to the churches and great cathedrals of Boston. Empty bottles and bright-colored bits of paper lay on the ground, and she recalled hearing that a festival of some kind had taken place here recently.

She crossed her arms and looked around, wondering what Mrs. Braddock found that was so picturesque in Santa Maria del Pueblo. Samantha thought only an overheated imagination could find it picturesque. There was no museum, concert hall, or tea parlor. Men could go to saloons, but where could a woman go?

"My sister is very sick. You give me some money, señora?"

Samantha looked down and saw a slim little Mexican boy with a long sad face and big brown eyes. He was barefoot, wearing rags, and Samantha was astonished to see him standing there.

"You give me money—we send for the doctor," the boy said, clasping his hands together and gazing imploringly into her eyes. "Please help, señora. God will repay you a hundred thousand times."

Samantha thought he was beautiful. Smiling, she opened her purse and dropped a few coins into his palm, and he brought his eyes close to the coins, counting them carefully.

"Thank you, señora," he said joyfully, his white teeth sparkling in the sun. "You are most kind. I have never seen you before, I do not think so. Are you new in this town?"

"I live on the Army post."

Paco extended his arm across the square. "Have you ever been to our famous church?"

"I'm not a Catholic," Samantha replied.

"You do not have to be a Catholic to go to our church. It is a very holy and great church. The Virgin herself appeared here to Padre Fernando many years ago when this was just a desert. This whole town is here only because of the Virgin. They say if you go inside and pray to the Virgin from deep in your heart, the Virgin will answer your prayer. I bet there is something you want very much, yes? Well, you go inside, and the Virgin will give it to you. Come on, I take you there."

The boy grabbed Samantha's hand and dragged her across the square. She didn't resist, and was amused by the boy's antics. The closer she came to the church, the uglier it became. It was made of adobe like everything else in the town, and the proportions looked wrong.

Paco stopped in front of the door. "You go inside now, señora. You pray to the Virgin and she will help you."

Samantha shook her head nervously. "No, I don't think so. I'm not a believer, I'm afraid."

"You do not believe in God?" Paco asked, his eyes wide open with incredulity.

"I don't know what I believe."

Paco looked up at her. "You would believe if you had seen Father Fernando, because he had the stigmata. He bleed from his hands and his feets and his body, like *Jesús Cristo*. He was a very holy man, and the Virgin speak with him *right here*."

"Did you ever see the stigmata yourself?" Samantha asked.

"Oh, no, señora. Father Fernando has been with God for a very long time. But my grandmother, my *abuela*, saw Father Fernando and the stigmata. She say he glowed as if he was made of gold."

Their superstitions are what keep them poor, Samantha thought, looking down at Paco. *This is why they have to beg.*

Paco noticed her hesitation. "I take you," he said.

His slim fingers grasped her hand and before she knew what was happening she was being pulled into the church. She passed through the portals and found herself plunged into darkness, except for dim light surrounding the statue of the Virgin at the far end of the church.

She became aware that people were praying in the pews, and could hear their whispers. The atmosphere was mysterious and a little frightening. The boy let her hand go.

"Where are you?" she asked.

There was no answer. Evidently he'd gone. She wanted to leave too, but somehow couldn't bring herself to turn around and walk out the door. The church was odd and interesting. It might be something to tell the people back in Boston about next time she wrote home.

She looked at the statue of the Virgin, and thought she might as well take a closer look while she was in the church. She walked down the aisle, passing men and women hunched over in pews, rattling prayer beads. The church was nearly deserted. *How odd that a whole town would be built around a popular delusion.*

She approached the statue, and a few women in black shawls prayed on their knees in front of it. Samantha had visited many fine art museums in her day, and could see that the statue was

cheap, gaudy, and sentimental, even with an artificial tear
flowing out of the Virgin's eye. *How can anybody believe
this nonsense?*

She was about to turn and leave when she remembered what
Paco told her: the Virgin would answer her prayer if she prayed
hard enough.

What the hell, she said to herself. She closed her eyes and
thought: *Please let me go back to Boston*, and as those words
passed through her mind, she saw images of Beacon Hill, the
Common, and Boston harbor. She became filled with a deep
and terrible homesickness. How wonderful it'd be to see her
friends again. There was so much to do, so many interesting
places to go, and plenty of stimulating companions in Boston.
I want to go home so badly, she thought.

She opened her eyes, and the time-worn plaster statue stood
in front of her, arms extended. Samantha shrugged and turned
around, walking toward the door of the church and the light of
the hot desert afternoon.

The Apache band rode across a flat expanse of desert baking
in the sun. In their center was the wagon loaded with stolen
goods, bouncing and rocking over the uneven ground, and the
horses pulling the wagon frothed at their mouths and strained
mightily with their load.

Coyotero sat erectly astride his horse at the head of the band,
scabs of blood covering the spots where he'd been cut by Lobo.
It had been another successful raid, and he'd only lost a few
warriors. They were lying head down on the saddles of their
horses at the rear of the war party.

Coyotero was in a rotten mood. He felt humiliated by Lobo,
and his confidence in himself was shaken because he'd never
tasted the bitter gall of defeat before. With shame in his heart
he recalled how he'd stood quivering with Lobo's knife in his
throat, and he'd been certain he was going to die, but Lobo had
given him his life back, and that was the most embarrassing
part of it all. Now he was beholden to Lobo, whom he hated.

Tomorrow he'd fight Lobo again, and this time he couldn't
lose. Somehow he'd have to be stronger and faster than ever,
and he'd try no more fancy tricks, tossing his knife from one
hand to the other. Tomorrow he'd steel himself and kill Lobo

before everyone in the tribe. Tomorrow there'd be no mistakes.

Farther back, in the midst of Apache warriors singing victory songs, Stone was wondering when he'd be able to get away from his captors and go to San Antone to look for Marie.

He'd been flabbergasted when Ralph McIntyre had said he thought he'd seen Marie in San Antone. After showing the photograph all across the frontier for four years, somebody finally recognized her! He'd been getting discouraged by his fruitless search during the past several months, and even had thought about forgetting Marie and settling down with somebody else, but now his hope was renewed.

He glanced at Peggy McIntyre riding the horse next to him, and she sat in her saddle listlessly, a blank expression on her face. The attack on her home had been so sudden and tragic that she'd gone mad, and Stone wondered if something similar might've happened to Marie.

Sherman's Army marauded through South Carolina, passing directly through their area, burning, pillaging, and destroying. Perhaps Marie's mind had cracked under the strain. Maybe that's why she'd never left a message for him.

He'd been confused and demoralized before arriving at the McIntyre ranch, but now at last saw the possibility of getting some answers. The mystery would be solved if Marie was in San Antone. He hoped he'd find her there.

On Stone's other side, Lobo sat in his saddle, thinking about the Owl Sickness. He believed it had slowed him down during his fight with Coyotero, and nearly cost his life a few times. Once, when Coyotero had attacked him, Coyotero's knife narrowly missed Lobo's throat, and Lobo had a vision of the Ghost Pony. The image lasted only a moment or two, and Lobo had gone on to win the fight, but it had been very disturbing.

Tomorrow he'd fight Coyotero again, and he needed help against the Owl Sickness. He knew of an old medicine woman in the tribe, Mountain Blossom was her name, and he'd seek her counsel as soon as he returned. Maybe she could cure him of the Owl Sickness, not just for his good, but for the good of the entire tribe.

Lobo believed Coyotero was an evil man and a danger to the tribe. He hated Coyotero and always had, even before Coyotero married his sister. He'd never liked the way Coyotero flouted the traditions of the people, traditions that had maintained and strengthened the people since the dawn of time.

Lobo couldn't understand why the spirits gave so much to Coyotero, while Coyotero gave so little to them. Somehow it didn't seem fair, but a person could never understand the spirits. They lived by their own rules and had their own work to do.

Somehow I must kill Coyotero tomorrow, he thought. *There can be no other way.*

Juanita rode on the other side of Lobo, and she was deeply troubled. She was a captive of the dreaded Apaches, and thought they'd either kill her or make her their slave.

She didn't want either possibility. Somehow, no matter what she did, her situation became worse. She'd thought life had been bad enough with Rodrigo. He'd beaten her and used her in all sorts of terrible ways, but at least he'd been a Mexican. The Apaches were worse than animals, in her opinion. They lived like rats in the desert, tortured their prisoners horribly, and didn't believe in *Jesús Cristo*.

She glanced sideways at John Stone, her golden earrings glittering in the sun. *The gringo is my only chance,* she thought. If John Stone escaped, surely he'd take her with him. He wouldn't leave her to the cruelties of the Apaches. He was a good man, even if he was a gringo.

Everything happen to me, she said to herself, pinching her lips together in frustration. *I cannot do nothing right.*

The cavalry patrol rode onto the main grounds of the McIntyre ranch, and before them stretched mass devastation. All the buildings were burned to the ground, and only charred pieces of wood and blackened metal fixtures remained. Buzzards circled in the sky overhead, their meal interrupted by the arrival of the cavalry.

Lieutenant Lowell held up his hand, and the patrol stopped behind him. Everyone stared at the man tied upside down to the wagon wheel, his head roasted and burst apart over the ashes of a fire, his limbs stiff from rigor mortis, and he'd been partially eaten by the buzzards.

A sweet stench was in the air, and Lieutenant Lowell felt sick to his stomach. He climbed down from his horse and walked to where the main ranch building had been.

He'd been here before and knew the McIntyres fairly well. They'd had a beautiful home, and now it was all gone. Old Ralph McIntyre should've heeded the warnings, but it was too late now.

Tim Connors and Sergeant McFeeley followed him along with several of the men and the two Apache scouts, Chinchi and Blanco. They approached the destroyed building and saw burned bodies in the debris, some with arrows sticking out of them, and they too had been torn by the sharp beaks of the buzzards.

Lieutenant Lowell felt a powerful rage build inside him. It was a terrible atrocity, the worst he'd seen in his year on the frontier. He recalled the McIntyre women, mother and daughter, and assumed they were in the scorched remains of the building. Near him, Chinchi and Blanco were talking.

"What're they saying?" Lieutenant Lowell asked.

Tim Connors conferred with the Apaches in their language, then turned to Lieutenant Lowell. "They're wondering who did this, because the McIntyres always had been good friends of their people."

"Not anymore," Licutenant Lowell said. "We're going after whoever did this. Take the scouts and pick up their trail."

Tim Connors spoke with the Apache scouts, and they walked off, looking for tracks to follow. Lieutenant Connors stepped back to his horse, took out a thin cigar, and lit it. The buzzards circled overhead, squawking angrily at those who'd disturbed their meal.

Lieutenant Lowell puffed his cigar and waited impatiently for his scouts to pick up the trail of the Apache war party. He sipped some water from his canteen, rolled it around in his mouth, and swallowed it. Out of the corner of his eye, he saw the unlucky soul tied to the wagon wheel. *What kind of people would do something like that?*

Lieutenant Lowell thought there was something diabolical and inhuman about the Apaches. He knew they were fighting for their land, but why the atrocities? What kind of mind could conceive of tying a man upside down and building a fire under his head?

His men shuffled around the site, muttering angrily and swearing revenge. Many of them had met the McIntyres and liked them. Some of the older soldiers had known the McIntyre children since they were small.

Tim Connors returned with the Apache scouts. "We've found their trail, sir. There was about twenty or thirty of 'em." He pointed west. "They went thataway."

"Saddle up!" Lieutenant Lowell shouted to his men. "Let's go—we're moving out!"

"But, sir," Tim Connors protested, "the Apaches're prob'ly on their way to their camp. There'll be a lot more of them than us."

"We'll worry about that when we get there," Lieutenant Lowell replied.

"I think you ought to send for reinforcements, sir."

Lieutenant Lowell realized that would be the prudent thing to do. He could be criticized afterward if he didn't take the appropriate precautions, but it'd be wonderful if he could find the Apache camp with his patrol and overwhelm the Apaches in a hellbent-for-leather cavalry charge.

Lieutenant Lowell wondered who to send to Fort Kimball. He didn't think any of his soldiers could make the trip alone, and he needed Sergeant McFeeley with him. He didn't trust his Apache scouts, so that left Tim Connors.

"Think you can make the trip?" he asked Connors.

"I'll damn well try, sir."

Connors wheeled his horse and spurred him hard. The horse galloped away, heading back in the direction of Fort Kimball.

Lieutenant Lowell climbed onto his horse and turned it toward the trail left by the Apaches. Sergeant McFeeley shouted orders and the patrol formed up behind him. The trooper carrying the guidon took his place beside Lieutenant Lowell. Sergeant McFeeley rode toward Lieutenant Lowell and saluted.

"The patrol is ready to move out, sir!"

Lieutenant Lowell raised his arm in the air. "Forward ho!" he hollered.

The two Apache scouts, Chinchi and Blanco, galloped forward to take the point. Lieutenant Lowell and the rest of the patrol followed them out of the yard, leaving behind the ruins of the McIntyre ranch, and the buzzards dropped down from the sky to finish their feast.

• • •

Miguel pointed toward a green cluster of trees and bushes straight ahead. "That is the water hole," he said to Antonio.

Antonio's lips were cracked and his mouth was dry. An hour ago he'd finished the last drop of water in his canteen. "Go forward and see that it is safe."

Miguel spurred his horse, who moved eagerly toward the water, his ears pricked up, his tongue hanging out of his mouth. They were traveling over open country dotted with bushes, trees, and cactuses. Miguel's eyes swept back and forth, looking for odd shapes and unusual movements. He held his pistol in his hands as he peered into the desert foliage, knowing that an entire army of Apaches could be around him and he might not even see them.

A bird flew past, and everything seemed normal. Miguel looked down at the ground, and there were no tracks, but if Apaches were going to spring an ambush, they wouldn't leave tracks.

He moved closer to the water hole, and couldn't wait to put his mouth into it. His horse quickened his pace, snorting and shaking his head. The water was directly ahead, shimmering in the sunlight. Miguel pulled back the reins, and the horse whinnied, because he didn't want to stop when he was so close to water. Miguel pulled harder, and the horse came to a stop reluctantly.

Miguel looked around once more, examining the bushes. Everything seemed all right. He took off his sombrero, turned around in his saddle, and waved his sombrero at the others, signaling that they should come on.

They saw his signal and advanced. Miguel placed his sombrero back on his head and let his horse walk the final twenty yards to the water hole. The animal moved swiftly and lowered his head. When he came to the water he touched his big hairy lips to it and slurped.

Miguel climbed down from the horse, looked behind him, and saw Antonio and the others approaching. Miguel took one last look around, holstered his pistol, and got down on his hands and knees, sinking his face toward the water, drinking noisily like the horse.

To his rear, he could hear the advancing hoofbeats of Antonio and the others. He drank deeply, the cool sweet liquid flowing down his throat. When he had his fill, he unscrewed the top of his canteen and pushed it beneath the surface of the water, watching the bubbles erupt and break the surface.

He heard a shout behind him. Spinning around, he was shocked to see Apaches covered with dirt leaping up at Antonio and the others, swinging hatchets and firing pistols! They'd been hiding in the ground, buried beneath the surface, and Miguel's heart pounded furiously in his chest as he dropped his canteen and reached for his pistol. A shot rang out behind him, and he felt a sharp hot pain in his back. Spinning around, he saw two Apaches running toward him, one with a rifle in his hands, the other carrying a hatchet.

Miguel's legs gave out underneath him, and he dropped to his knees. He wanted to shoot the Apaches, but didn't have the strength to raise his pistol. A volley of shots fired behind him, men screamed, and the Apache with the hatchet let out a war cry and swung his weapon at Miguel's head.

Miguel felt the world split apart. The force of the blow hurled him to the ground, where he lay still, his blood trailing off into the water hole where his horse continued to drink noisily.

Coyotero and his raiding party rode into their camp, singing victory songs and carrying their booty. Some brandished new rifles, others wore coats and hats that had belonged to the McIntyres, a few wore necklaces and earrings, and several herded the stolen horses.

The Apache women and children ran toward their men, dazzled by the influx of new riches. Stone sat on his horse and stared wide-eyed at the celebration. He'd never seen an Indian camp before, and watched children jump up and down around their fathers, who tossed them clothing and baubles.

Some of the women got down on their knees and chanted a song of thanks, raising their arms to the sky. The warriors were returning heroes, and sat proudly on their horses. Leading the way was Coyotero, his chin high, bouncing up and down in his saddle. Stone could see great wealth coming to the community. It was the same kind of wild joy as if there'd been a gold strike in a mining town.

Some of the warriors broke out the bottles of whiskey they'd stolen from the McIntyre home. They pulled the corks out of the bottles, upended them, and gulped down the fiery liquid. Lobo pointed forward to an old man emerging from one of the wickiups and said to Stone: "That is my father."

Jacinto pulled himself to his full height in front of the wicki-up and looked at the scene before him. He saw the horses, rifles, clothes, pots and pans, and other material goods. It had been a successful raid, but not for everybody. At the rear of the war party were the dead warriors heads down over their saddles, their wives howling in grief around them.

Casualties couldn't be avoided on raids. The life of a warrior was hazardous, and the Ghost Pony always was in the shadows. Few warriors died of old age, especially in recent years when traditional Apache land had been taken over increasingly by the white eyes.

Coyotero rode toward him, and Jacinto wondered where the raid had taken place. He didn't see Red Feather and then his heart quickened when his eyes fell on Lobo, a fresh wound on his cheek.

Jacinto normally was composed and deliberate at all times, but he lost it for a few moments when he saw his beloved son riding amid the returning warriors. Jacinto took a step forward, but caught himself. First he'd have to greet Coyotero, leader of the raid.

Coyotero stopped his horse in front of Jacinto and dismounted. He walked toward the old man and bowed. "We have returned, great Chief," he said. Reaching into his shirt, he pulled out a pearl necklace with a cameo pendant attached to it. "This is for you, a token of our esteem."

A half smile on his face, he handed the necklace to Jacinto, who held it in his hands and gazed at it, his brow wrinkled. The necklace looked familiar. "Where did you get this thing?" he asked.

"On our raid, great Chief."

"Where was your raid?"

"A ranch where the white eyes live."

Meanwhile, other members of the raiding party dismounted and gathered around Coyotero and Jacinto. There was a terrific amount of noise as women and children shouted gleefully.

Jacinto looked into Coyotero's eyes and was afraid to ask the question, but did so anyway. "Which ranch?"

"I told you," Coyotero replied evasively, "a ranch where the white eyes live."

Lobo approached from the side. "It was the McIntyre ranch," he said to his father. "Coyotero has killed your blood brother."

Jacinto's eyes widened for a moment. He threw the cameo pendant to the ground, drew his knife out of its sheath, and took a step toward Coyotero.

"I do not fight old men," Coyotero said derisively.

Jacinto advanced to within striking distance of Coyotero, raised his arm in the air, and drove the knife down toward Coyotero's breast, but Coyotero casually lifted his hand and took hold of Jacinto's wrist, stopping the downward movement of the knife.

"I told you—I do not fight old men."

Jacinto's face was inches from Coyotero's. "You have killed my blood brother!"

"He was a white eyes, and a white eyes cannot ever be a blood brother to an Apache. To think otherwise is to be a foolish old man."

Jacinto quivered with rage at Coyotero and his own impotence. Unable to overcome Coyotero's strength, he had no choice but to surrender. Coyotero let him go, and Jacinto felt humiliated before his tribe. He returned his knife to its sheath and tried to retain as much dignity as he could.

"You have no honor," he said to Coyotero. "You must go."

"Very well—I will go," Coyotero said, "and with me will come the warriors who want what I can give them." He raised his modern new rifle in the air, to indicate what he could give them. "I do not think many warriors will want to stay with you, who can offer them nothing but the friendship of the white eyes, a friendship that has never meant anything but pain to our people."

"Where is Red Feather?" Jacinto asked.

"He is dead."

"I do not see him. How did he die?"

"On the raid."

Lobo stepped forward. "That is a lie. I was visiting the

McIntyre ranch when Lobo and his warriors attacked, and Red Feather was not among them."

Jacinto looked around at the warriors. They weren't cheering and celebrating anymore. Something serious was taking place, and they had solemn expressions on their faces. Jacinto's eyes fell on Eagle Claw, whom he'd always trusted.

"What happened to Red Feather?" he asked.

Eagle Claw hesitated, because he knew there'd be trouble if he spoke. Coyotero turned to him, and he thought Coyotero might attack him if he told the truth, but he didn't dare show any fear of Coyotero in front of the other warriors who knew the true story. It would be better to die than be considered a coward.

"Coyotero killed Red Feather," he said. "They had an argument and Coyotero took Red Feather by the throat, and choked him."

Jacinto looked at Coyotero. "You are an evil man. The blood of a great medicine man is on your hands."

Coyotero laughed. "A great fool, you mean. That is all he was."

"The mountains spirits will punish you for what you have done, Coyotero. You may be a great warrior, but you are not greater than the mountain spirits."

Coyotero raised his stolen rifle again. "They have rewarded me, not punished me for what I have done. I am a greater medicine man than Red Feather ever was. The success of my raid attests to that. And as for you, esteemed Chief, when is the last time you ever have led such a successful raid?"

Jacinto trembled with rage. "You have murdered my friends!"

"Not all of them," Coyotero replied coolly.

Coyotero turned and walked back into the crowd. Jacinto's vision wasn't acute anymore, and he could only see Coyotero swaggering toward some people on horseback at the edge of the gathering.

Coyotero continued to make his way toward Stone, Juanita, and Peggy. He raised his arms and lifted Peggy out of her saddle, cradling her in his arms as he carried her back to Jacinto.

Now Jacinto could discern who she was, and a wave of tenderness passed over him. He'd first seen her when she was an infant, and now she was numbed and staring, obviously in a state of shock.

Coyotero stopped in front of Jacinto. "You see, great Chief, I did not kill them all. I saved this one. She will be my slave."

"No!" Jacinto replied forcefully. "She is the daughter of my blood brother and is under my protection!"

"I have captured her," Coyotero retorted. "The white bitch belongs to me."

"Never," said the deep strong voice of Lobo.

All eyes turned to him, and he stepped out of the crowd, a long swathe of dried blood on his cheek. "The entire story has not yet been told," he said. "Coyotero and I fought at the McIntyre ranch. I could have killed him, but spared his life because last time we fought he spared mine. Now we are even. We have agreed to fight tomorrow at noon, and in that fight the loser will not be spared. If Coyotero wins, he takes his captives. If I win, they will be mine." He turned to Coyotero. "Is that not so?"

"It is so," Coyotero said.

"If it is so, the white eyes girl is not yours yet. She should remain under the protection of our chief, until the fight." Lobo turned and appealed to the crowd. "Is that not the just thing to do?"

They nodded their heads, and Coyotero's face became dark with anger. Lowering Peggy to the ground, he pushed her toward Jacinto, who took her hand gently. She seemed not to know where she was.

"It is decided," Jacinto said as Peggy stood at his side, staring sightlessly at the gathering of Apaches in front of her. "The fight will take place tomorrow when the sun is directly overhead. I have spoken."

Jacinto turned and led Peggy toward his wickiup, where his wife, Wind Woman, was waiting. The crowd dispersed amid grumbling and confusion. Great new wealth had come into their tribe suddenly, but also great new trouble. Everyone knew that life in the tribe would never be the same again after Coyotero's raid on the McIntyre ranch.

• • •

It was late afternoon and the sun cast long shadows over Fort Kimball as a lone rider in buckskin made his way toward the command post.

He was Tim Connors, the old scout, and a rag bandage was tied around his left bicep. Dusty and pale, he slumped over on his saddle. A guard in front of the command post ran forward to guide his horse toward the hitching rail.

"What happened to you?" the guard asked.

"Apaches," Connors replied wearily.

Connors climbed down from his horse and mounted the steps in front of the adobe headquarters building. He crossed the veranda and opened the door. Sergeant Foley sat behind the desk.

"Where's the colonel?" Connors asked.

"Home havin' supper."

Connors turned around, to walk to Colonel Braddock's quarters, when he was struck by dizziness. Sergeant Foley arose from behind the desk, rushing toward Connors and holding him steady.

"I think you need the doc," Foley said.

"Got to talk to the colonel."

"I'll get him for you."

Sergeant Foley helped Connors to a chair, then ran out to get Colonel Braddock. Connors took a deep breath, then rolled himself a cigarette. Three Apaches on horseback had chased him for an hour and fired many arrows at him. One of the arrows had gone through his arm, but Connors pulled it out and kept going. The Apaches gave up their chase finally, and Connors was able to bandage his wound, but he'd lost a lot of blood.

He leaned back in the chair and puffed his cigarette. *I'm gittin' too old for this shit,* he said to himself.

He closed his eyes and passed out, the cigarette dangling out of the corner of his mouth. A few minutes later footsteps stirred him to consciousness. The door opened and Colonel Braddock entered the office, followed by Sergeant Foley.

"What happened?" said Colonel Braddock.

Connors tried to get to his feet, to render the proper salute, but Colonel Braddock pushed him back into the chair.

"You can tell me from where you're sitting."

Connors looked up at the colonel. "About thirty Apaches attacked the McIntyre ranch and burned it to the ground. Everybody there was massacred. Lieutenant Lowell is pursuin', and he asks fer reinforcements, sir."

Colonel Braddock knitted his brows together. He'd always been afraid the McIntyre ranch would be attacked someday Thirty warriors would outnumber Lieutenant Lowell's patrol, and Lieutenant Lowell would be hard-pressed if he ran into them. The only thing to do was reinforce Lowell as soon as possible.

"Do you think you can ride?" Colonel Braddock asked Connors.

"A good meal and a little rest, and I could go anywheres, sir."

Colonel Braddock turned to Sergeant Foley. "Tell Captain Danforth to report here immediately. And when you're finished with that, ask Dr. Lantz to have a look at Connors here."

Sergeant Foley walked swiftly out of the room, and Colonel Braddock entered his office, closing the door. He approached his map table and looked down at the **X** that marked the McIntyre ranch. He thought of the McIntyre women, and how they must've died. It wouldn't have been pretty.

Clasping his hands behind his back, he studied the map. He wanted to lead the expedition that would go to Lieutenant Lowell's aid, but he had more to worry about than Lieutenant Lowell. Captain Danforth would have to go. Captain Danforth was his toughest and most experienced Apache fighter.

Several minutes later there was a knock on his door, and he turned around. "Come in!"

The door opened and Captain Danforth entered. He was short, stocky, forty years old, wearing a long flowing rust-colored mustache. An unmarried officer, he'd risen from the ranks, winning a battlefield commission at Antietam.

He came to attention in front of Colonel Braddock and saluted.

"I suppose Sergeant Foley told you the news," Colonel Braddock said.

"Yes, sir."

"I want you to take Troop F immediately and reinforce Lieutenant Lowell. Connors will be your guide. Are there any questions?"

"No, sir."

Captain Danforth saluted, performed a smart about-face, and marched out of the office. Colonel Braddock looked out the window at the clear blue sky. He knew that Lieutenant Lowell was relatively inexperienced, and wondered if he'd got himself into trouble yet.

I hope Danforth reaches him in time, Colonel Braddock thought.

Lieutenant Lowell and his patrol stopped on a rocky plateau cut by a winding stream. The two Apache scouts clambered over the plateau, jabbering with each other, while the troopers watered their horses and filled their canteens. The empty wagon, abandoned by the Apache raiders, was near the stream.

Lieutenant Lowell sat on the hard rock, his knees in the air, smoking a cigar and watching the sun dip toward the horizon. The Apache scouts had lost the trail and were trying to pick it up. Lieutenant Lowell was eager to get moving. He didn't want the Apache raiders to get away.

He kept thinking about General George Armstrong Custer, who'd won a great victory over the Cheyenne Indians in the Battle of the Washita on Thanksgiving Day a year ago. Custer had come upon a Cheyenne village of 75 lodges under Chief Black Kettle and attacked immediately, killing 105 Indians and capturing 53 women and children, and Chief Black Kettle himself had been among the casualties. The battle had been publicized throughout the country, and made Custer even more famous than he was already.

Indians in villages usually ran when attacked by cavalry, just as the Cheyenne had run in the Battle of the Washita. The power of cavalry was too much for them. A determined attack was everything.

Lieutenant Lowell wished he could find Jacinto's village and do the same thing. Then he'd be famous too, and become a captain, wearing two bars on his shoulder boards instead of one, becoming a troop commander. Then maybe Samantha would take his military career more seriously. He imagined she'd be proud to be the wife of a famous officer.

His reverie was interrupted by the approach of his two
Apache scouts, and they didn't appear happy. Lieutenant
Lowell rose to greet them.

"They have split up," Chinchi said. "They have gone in many
ways." He turned around and pointed his fingers in several
directions. "They will join up together somewhere and return
to camp."

Lieutenant Lowell wished he had Tim Connors there, to
advise him about what course to take next.

"Where do you think their camp is?" Lieutenant Lowell
asked.

"There are many places to make camp," Chinchi said with
a shrug. "Could be anywhere."

"You know where the camps are, don't you?"

Chinchi nodded.

"We'll check them one by one, then."

Chinchi looked at Blanco, then back to Lieutenant Lowell.
"But there are many camps."

"We've got no other choice, and maybe while we're search-
ing we can pick up their trail." Lieutenant Lowell turned
around. "Sergeant McFeeley!"

"Yes, sir!"

"Form up the patrol! We're moving out!"

Lobo paused outside the wickiup of Mountain Blossom, the
old medicine woman. From inside, he could hear her chanting.
This was the way she spent most of her time, in prayer. She
was considered a great holy woman, and Apaches from other
tribes often came to confer with her.

"Mountain Blossom," he said. "It is Lobo, son of Jacinto,
come to speak with you."

She continued chanting for another minute or two, then it
was silent for a while. Finally she said: "Enter, Lobo."

Lobo bent down and crawled through the entrance hole. It
was dark inside the wickiup, and Mountain Blossom sat beside
the flickering fire pit. She was ancient, with deep wrinkles in
her face, and scraggly gray hair. Lobo sat opposite her and
bowed.

"I have the Owl Sickness," he said.

"How did it come upon you?"

Lobo described seeing the owl when he was on his way to the water hole, and how it flew past him. "Tomorrow at noon I must fight Coyotero, and I am afraid the Owl Sickness will make me weak and cause me to be killed."

She closed her eyes and hummed softly for a while, then opened her eyes and spoke: "Lie on your back with your head facing east."

Lobo did as she requested, his head toward the entrance to the wickiup.

"Close your eyes and spread out your arms."

She began to hum, thrusting her hand into a leather bag, taking out a handful of sacred pollen, sprinkling it over Lobo. Then she reached into another bag and removed a handful of small quartz crystals, dropping them onto his face. She passed her hands over his body, then sat beside him and chanted in a low monotonous drone.

Lobo went limp on the ground. There was a buzzing in his head that matched the sound of her chanting. He felt himself falling asleep. A vision of the desert passed before his eyes. He saw an enormous expanse of country—massive buttes and valleys—streaked with the white of long meandering dry washes. Buzzards flew in circles against the blue sky, synchronized to the sound of Mountain Blossom's chanting, while beneath them, galloping wildly across a sandy plateau, was the Ghost Pony, his long white mane undulating in the breeze.

Near Jacinto's wickiup, Stone and Juanita sat cross-legged on the ground, eating stewed horsemeat out of wooden bowls. Juanita looked around suspiciously at Apache warriors and women in the vicinity. Perico, the nephew of Lobo, sat on the ground ten feet away from Stone and Juanita and couldn't take his eyes off them.

"I am afraid of these people," Juanita said to Stone. "We have got to get out of here."

"I don't think we'd get far," Stone replied. "Apaches are supposed to be the best trackers in the world."

"We must try to escape somehow. Think of something, will you? I thought you were supposed to be a smart gringo."

"If Lobo wins the fight, they'll let us go. If he doesn't, maybe Jacinto can protect us. Otherwise we might have to fight our way out of here."

They heard a commotion at the far end of the camp and turned their heads in that direction. Stone saw warriors on horseback returning to camp, and they had two prisoners with them, their hands bound behind their backs, and also on horseback.

"*Ay Dios!*" Juanita said, staring in shock at the prisoners.

"What's wrong?" Stone asked her.

"It is Antonio," she replied, "Rodrigo's brother, and he is with Luis, another member of the band!"

Stone and Juanita followed the others gathering around the returning warriors and their prisoners. There were twenty warriors with the horses, saddles, and possessions of the Mexican bandits.

Luis looked more dead than alive. He had a huge bloody bruise on his forehead where he'd been struck by an Apache war club, and his head hung low. He was dazed and confused, because he had a brain concussion. His shirt was covered with blood.

Antonio also was bloodied, with cuts on his face and his clothing torn. He'd put up a hard fight but they'd taken him alive. He knew what Apaches did to their prisoners, and hoped he could take it like a man.

Children and women gathered around him, jeering and spitting. Some of them threw stones that bounced off his body and the top of his head. He ducked, but couldn't avoid all the projectiles. The warriors who'd captured him rode proudly, for their ambush had been successful. They sat stiffly in their saddles, accepting the cheers of their families.

In pain, and fearful of the terrible death that he knew the Apaches would inflict upon him, Antonio was astonished to see a familiar face in the crowd. He blinked, because he thought he might be dreaming, but then realized it was Juanita, Rodrigo's woman, standing next to a tall, powerfully built gringo.

Juanita made no sign that she recognized him, and he didn't respond to her either.

The Apache warriors stopped their horses and climbed down. Then they roughly pulled Antonio and Luis to the ground. Antonio's arms and hands were tied tightly behind his back and he couldn't do anything to protect himself from the women and children who crowded around him, screaming insults, punching, and kicking.

He gritted his teeth as he fell beneath their cruel punishment, and then he was on the ground; they kicked him repeatedly in the face. He felt his nose split apart and his teeth smashed back into his mouth but then an old woman whacked him on the temple with a length of firewood and he passed out, numb at last to the cascade of blows falling upon him.

Samantha sat at her desk, scratching her pen on a sheet of white paper. She'd decided not to leave her husband, and instead stay at Fort Kimball, maintaining her sanity by writing about her experiences.

She'd got the idea while in Santa Maria del Pueblo earlier in the day. Her encounter with the little beggar boy and her experience in the quaint old church had stimulated her imagination. She'd realized that people back east could never imagine a town like Santa Maria del Pueblo, so she thought she'd write about it in a diary that she hoped to publish someday. She'd also write about Fort Kimball, military life in general, the people she met, the flora and fauna of the desert, and she thought it'd make interesting reading for armchair travelers back in Boston.

It grew darker in the room as the sun sank toward the horizon. She was having difficulty reading her writing, and thought she'd light the lamp, when she became aware of a major activity outside.

She arose from her desk and walked to the window. Outside on the parade ground, a large number of cavalry soldiers were riding off into the desert. It was a stirring sight, the guidons fluttering in the breeze and sergeants barking commands as the sun sank behind the mountain range to the west of the fort.

I wonder where they're going, she thought, and then realized it'd be an interesting military activity to describe for the folks back east. Turning around, she rushed back to the desk and sat down. She picked up her pen, paused for a moment, and then the sound of her stylus scratching against the paper could be heard, while from the distance resounded the hoofbeats of cavalry mounts and the blowing of the bugler, as Captain Danforth and Troop F took the field.

Captain Danforth rode at the head of the column, with his executive officer to his left and Tim Connors to his right. His bugler and the corporal carrying the Troop F guidon were behind him.

Captain Danforth wasn't too popular with his men, because he drove them hard. He didn't mix easily with other officers because he hadn't graduated from West Point or any other institution of higher learning. He was essentially a loner, a heavy drinker and carouser with a mean temper and a violent nature. All he knew was fighting, and everyone respected him for that.

Troop F rode onto the desert, and Captain Danforth scowled. He knew what his mission really was: to save the ass of a young fancypants West Point officer who'd got himself in trouble. Lieutenant Lowell wasn't his favorite person, but duty was duty. Captain Danforth would do whatever he could to find him. He intended to push his men all night to make up for lost time.

The sun disappeared behind the mountains and a coyote howled in the distance as Troop F rode across the darkening expanse of desert.

It was the middle of the night, and Antonio looked up at the stars. He wished he'd die quickly, but it didn't look as if it was going to be that way.

Green strips of rawhide bound him to the sharp spikes of a cactus plant, and as the rawhide dried and shrank, it pulled him more tightly against the spikes.

The spikes were sticking into his stomach, chest, and face, making him bleed, but this was only the beginning. It was dark and cool on the desert. In the morning when the sun came up, the thongs would pull him against the spikes and kill him.

It was going to be a slow painful death. Luis was the lucky one, nearly dead already, lying still on the ground several feet from Antonio. The Apaches had staked him to an anthill and smeared his eyes and lips with honey. The ants had been eating him up slowly all night, burrowing their way into his brain through his eyes, and into his throat, stomach, and lungs through his mouth. At first the screams had been horrible, and they'd gone on for hours, but now Luis was quiet. Occasionally a slight whimper would erupt out of his ant-clogged throat, but he was mostly gone.

Antonio knew he'd be gone soon too. He thought he was too young to die, but that wouldn't matter when the sun came up in the morning. The pain already was excruciating, hundreds of spikes sticking into him and getting deeper every second. In the morning they would pierce his throat, ribs, and heart slowly. He was half-insane, but made no sound. He was determined to die well, the way his brother Rodrigo would've expected.

He realized now that he shouldn't have come into Apache country. Love of Rodrigo and hatred of his killer had blinded him to the realities of the desert.

A wave of pain passed over him, and he nearly fainted. He thought about death and wondered if he'd go to hell, because he'd done many bad things in his life, stealing and killing. He wished a Catholic priest could give him absolution, but there were no Catholic priests around. All he could do was hug the spines of the cactus that bit into his soft flesh.

He remembered seeing Juanita when he'd ridden into the Apache camp. She'd been standing next to a tall gringo, and Antonio assumed he was the gringo who'd killed Rodrigo. Antonio had found him at last, but couldn't do anything about it.

A sigh passed between the lips of Luis, and Antonio wished Luis would die and get it over with. Antonio closed his eyes and recited the Rosary: "Holy Mary, Mother of God, pray for us sinners now and at the hour of our death."

He heard something rustle behind him. It might be a wolf or a bear who'd eat him alive, and his hair stood on end. He tried to move his head to see what it was, but the spikes of the cactus cut his skin. Someone was behind him, coming closer.

"Who's there?" he asked.

"Sssshhhhh," said Juanita. "Be quiet."

She carried a knife that she'd stolen from John Stone's boot, and cut the rawhide thongs that held Antonio to the cactus. Antonio felt the spikes withdraw from his skin. When she finished he took a step back and looked at her.

Her eyes gleamed in the moonlight as she stared at the hundreds of tiny wounds on his torso. She handed him the knife. "Take this and run for your life, Antonio."

He took the knife in his fist and staggered from side to side, barely able to hold himself up. "I ought to kill you," he said, raising the knife in the air.

She turned and ran away, leaving Antonio alone with the knife in his upraised hand. He didn't have enough strength to chase her. All he could do was stumble off into the desert, leaving Luis staked over the anthill, devoured by thousands of tiny ants.

It was three o'clock in the morning, and the crescent moon shone down on the ghostly ruins of the McIntyre ranch as Troop F came to a stop in the former front yard.

Captain Danforth sat on his saddle and coldly surveyed the scene. He was surprised it hadn't happened sooner. Ralph McIntyre had been an old fool. Anybody who trusted an Apache was crazy.

Tim Connors turned to Captain Danforth. "This is where I left Lieutenant Lowell, sir."

"Which way was he headed last time you saw him?"

Connors pointed west. "Thataway. He was followin' the trail left by the Apaches. We shouldn't have any trouble seein' it."

"Lead the way, Mr. Connors. We'll follow you."

Connors rode forward, looking down at the trampled earth over which the Apache raiders and Lieutenant Lowell's patrol had passed. Captain Danforth waited until Connors was about twenty yards away, then hollered: "Forward ho!"

Captain Danforth and Troop F followed Connors away from the McIntyre ranch and onto the open range. Captain Danforth peered ahead at the dim outlines of mountains and buttes in the distance. He knew Apaches didn't like to fight at night, and was certain Lieutenant Lowell had made camp somewhere. He hoped he could reach Lieutenant Lowell before the Apaches did, otherwise the Apaches would chew him up and spit him out.

Damn fool green West Pointer, Captain Danforth thought. *Just the kind that gets men killed for nothing.*

7

IN DEEP SLUMBER, Stone heard screaming. He awoke in a flash and reached for his Colts.

He was in a wickiup with Lobo, Juanita, Jacinto, Wind Woman, and Peggy McIntyre. Lobo sat up, his brow furrowed, listening.

"What's going on?" Stone asked.

"One of the prisoners has escaped."

Lobo pushed aside the length of hide that covered the entrance to the wickiup and went outside. It was dawn, and he saw a warrior carrying the cut thongs that had bound Antonio to the cactus.

"Someone freed the prisoner!" the warrior shouted. "There is a traitor among us!"

The warrior looked directly at Lobo as he said it, and the warrior was accompanied by a group of other warriors, all of whom had been with Coyotero on his raid against the McIntyre ranch. Lobo turned around and reentered the wickiup.

Meanwhile, Stone was pulling on his left boot. He reached for his right boot and noticed that his knife was missing from its sheath inside it. Juanita, on the other side of the wickiup, hid her head under her blankets and pretended to be asleep.

151

Lobo put on his headband and shirt and went outside again. Stone followed him, strapping on his gunbelts.

"My knife is missing," Stone said to Lobo. "It was in my boot, but it's not there now."

"Juanita took it," Lobo said. "During the night, I saw her."

"Why didn't you say something."

"I was curious to see what she would do."

A crowd of warriors, women, and children gathered in front of Jacinto's wickiup. Coyotero pushed through them and grabbed the cut thongs from the hand of the warrior who held them. Angrily he held the thongs in the air.

"No one would do such a thing except the white eyes!" he hollered. "They have freed their own!" He looked at Stone and sparks of flame shot out of his eyes. "You must die!"

Stone didn't say a word. He spread his legs and let his hands hang loose. If they came for him, a lot of them would bite the dust before they got him.

Jacinto came out of the tent and looked like a sleepy old man, his red headband crooked across his forehead. He drew himself up to his full height and rested his eyes upon Coyotero.

"You again," he said wearily. "You're always making noise about something."

"The white eyes have freed our prisoner! We demand a white eyes to take the place of the one who has been freed!"

Lobo pulled out his knife and looked at Coyotero. "All you're going to get is *this*!" He held the knife blade up in the air.

Coyotero whipped out his own knife and glowered at Lobo. They stared at each other in cold hatred for several seconds in silence, neither making a move.

Jacinto stepped between them. "The agreement was that you will fight at noon. As for the prisoner who escaped, he is of no importance. If someone wants to go after him, go ahead. I do not care. Lobo and Coyotero must stay apart until the time for their fight. Is that not so?"

He looked around at the people, and they nodded. Jacinto turned and bent over, crawling into his wickiup. Lobo and Coyotero continued to stare at each other, then Coyotero spat on the ground and plunged his knife into its sheath.

"You have spent much time with Mountain Blossom, but it

will not help you," Coyotero said. He turned and stalked away, followed by the warriors loyal to him.

Lobo watched him go, then drove his own knife into its sheath.

"What did he say?" Stone asked.

"Foolishness. Let us eat. We will need much strength for the day ahead."

Antonio shuffled across the desert, dragging his feet, Stone's knife fastened beneath his belt. Dried blood covered his face, throat, chest, and stomach from where the spikes of cactus had pierced his skin. He was weak from hunger, thirst, and loss of blood. He'd lost his hat when the Apaches captured him yesterday, and felt as if the sun were baking his brain.

All night he'd been wandering up and down hills, across silent valleys, past massive buttes towering up into the sky. Many times he thought he heard Apaches following him, and he hid in the chaparral, but no Apaches came.

Now it was morning, and he saw two buzzards circling over his head, squawking impatiently, waiting for him to fall. More than anything else in the world he wanted just one drink of water. He had no idea of where he was, but knew he was many miles from civilization.

"I'm going to die," he said aloud. "The buzzards and rats will eat my liver and gnaw on my bones."

The desert spun around him and he had to stop. He closed his eyes and when he opened them again he was on his knees. A prairie dog ran past him and he lunged for it, hoping to grab it and sink his teeth through its skin, so he could drink its blood.

He fell on his face in the sand, and the prairie dog was gone. Antonio lay on the sand for a long time, then realized he had to get moving if he wanted to live.

Laboriously he pushed himself to his feet, then teetered from side to side, breathing the hot desert air. His tongue was swollen and lips cracked, and every time he moved he felt excruciating pain all over his body. He peered ahead and was shocked to see two Apache warriors twenty yards in front of him, carrying rifles. They looked at him curiously, and he wondered if they were really there or if he was hallucinating. He rubbed his eyes, looked again, and saw that they were advancing toward him.

He reached to his belt and pulled out his knife, holding the blade up in the air. The Apaches stopped, and one of them threw him a canteen.

The canteen landed at his feet. Antonio dropped to his knees, picking up the canteen with trembling hands, unscrewing the cap and eagerly pressing the opening against his mouth.

He drank greedily although he knew he shouldn't drink too much at first, because it could make a man sick. Stopping himself, lowering the canteen, he screwed the lid back on and looked at the two Apaches, wondering why they hadn't killed him.

Then he noticed something behind the Apaches. He tried to focus and became aware of American cavalry soldiers in blue uniforms riding toward him.

He got to his feet, still holding on to the canteen tightly, staring in disbelief at the approaching column. The two Apaches smiled at him. "Maybe I have already died," Antonio said.

Antonio watched the cavalry soldiers come closer. Riding at their head was a young lieutenant with a black clipped mustache, flanked by the bugler and the corporal carrying the guidon flag, and behind them, in the column of twos, were soldiers in dark blue shirts and wide-brimmed cavalry hats.

The lieutenant raised his hand and the soldiers stopped behind him, sending forth a cloud of dust. The lieutenant rested his forearm on the horn of his saddle and leaned forward.

"What've we got here?" he asked.

"He looked like a Mexican," said Chinchi.

Lieutenant Lowell looked at Antonio. "Who are you?"

Antonio told him his name. "The Apaches captured me, but I have escaped."

"Were you in their camp?"

Antonio nodded.

"Can you lead us back to them?"

"I do not want to go there."

Lieutenant Lowell turned to Sergeant McFeeley. "Get this man something to ride and some food."

Sergeant McFeeley wheeled his horse around and rode back toward the rear of the column where the pack mules were. Lieutenant Lowell dismounted and walked toward Antonio. "Looks like you've had a bad time."

"They almost kill me," Antonio replied, raising the canteen to his mouth again, taking another swig.

"You'll be able to have your revenge, if you can lead us back there."

"I am not sure I know the way."

Chinchi was standing nearby with Blanco, pointing toward the ground. "We can follow his backtrail."

Lieutenant Lowell slapped Antonio on the shoulder, and Antonio blinked his eyes. He still couldn't be sure it wasn't a dream.

"When did you leave the Apache camp?" Lieutenant Lowell asked.

"Last night sometime."

"How did you escape?"

"A Mexican woman captive cut me loose."

Sergeant McFeeley returned with a mule, a straw hat, and a few squares of hardtack. Antonio put on the hat and the soldiers helped him climb onto the mule. He munched the hardtack as Lieutenant Lowell and Sergeant McFeeley remounted.

The cavalry patrol moved out, with Antonio riding the mule next to Lieutenant Lowell. Ahead of them, the two Apache scouts followed Antonio's backtrail into the desert.

Perico and several other boys sat on the ground watching John Stone and Lobo practice for the big fight.

They were beyond the last row of wickiups, at the edge of the desert, and several prominent warriors were nearby, studying the movements of each man.

Stone and Lobo circled each other, each carrying a knife, feinting, lunging, slashing at each other but making certain they wouldn't actually draw blood.

Lobo was working for speed and power, darting in and out, dancing from side to side, using the same tactics he'd used against Coyotero earlier. He knew that speed would be all-important, but he'd have to be strong too. Coyotero's sheer physical strength had been a significant factor in their previous encounters.

Stone was using an Apache knife given him by Lobo. It had a ten-inch blade sharp as a razor and a handle made out of the thigh bone of a bear. Stone got low, hunching his shoulders, moving the blade of the knife back and forth in front of him. He was pretending to be Coyotero, using the rushing and bullying tactics that Coyotero had employed.

Lobo kept maneuvering away from him, and Stone tried to cut off his retreat, charging forward to confront Lobo, but Lobo never was where Stone wanted him to be.

Stone knew he'd be in deep trouble if he were having a real fight with Lobo, because Lobo was much faster than Rodrigo and more skilled. Yet Stone was learning more about knife fighting than he'd ever known before. He knew he'd be better at it when he finished the practice.

Lobo was retreating again, and Stone thought he saw an opening. He charged, driving the point of his knife forward toward Lobo's stomach, but his knife cut thin air as Lobo jumped to the side and pressed the point of his own knife against Stone's left kidney.

Stone stopped cold in his tracks. Lobo had got him again. With a shrug, Stone stepped back and faced off with Lobo again. They looked at each other and their dance of death resumed, while above them, the sun climbed through the sky toward high noon.

Samantha sat at her desk, writing her account of a trip to the fort hospital that morning.

Dr. Lantz had shown her around, and it had been most depressing. Seven young soldiers were in bed, suffering from arrow and gunshot wounds, and one was nearly dead.

Samantha had sat at his bedside for a while, holding his hand, trying to comfort him. The soldier couldn't have been more than eighteen years old, and an arrow had been shot through his left lung. Dr. Lantz cut the arrow out two days ago, but the lung was destroyed and the soldier might not live much longer. His complexion was bluish-white and he hadn't regained full consciousness since the surgery.

Now Samantha was writing about it, venting her anger at the Apaches who made life unsafe for everybody in the Arizona Territory. Her plan was to send the story to one of the Boston newspapers, with the hope that they'd print it. She wanted the citizens back east to understand that Apaches weren't noble savages, as some of them might believe, but thieves, murderers, and fiends of the worst sort.

It was getting hot inside the hut, and Samantha felt weary. She brushed her golden hair back from her forehead and stood, walking to the window, looking out at the parade ground.

Several squads of soldiers drilled under the flaming sun, and she felt a layer of perspiration underneath her clothing. Every day was hot and sunny and she was so sick of it she wanted to scream.

Her mind drifted back to the Boston waterfront enshrouded in fog, the cool mist touching her cheeks, the great ships with their tall masts rocking in the swells.

She felt herself yearning for Boston, so homesick she wanted to cry. She wished she could return to that cool climate, and get away from the hot desert that was sucking her youth and strength.

I wish I could go home, she thought, recalling the prayer she'd made at the church in Santa Maria del Pueblo yesterday. *If only prayers came true.*

8

IT WAS HIGH noon, and every man, woman, and child in the tribe had gathered in a large circle in front of Jacinto's wickiup. Even sentries had left their posts to see the big fight between Lobo and Coyotero.

The crowd was about half for Lobo and the rest for Coyotero. Jacinto sat at the side of the circle nearest his wickiup, with the elders and leading medicine men and women of the tribe, and among them was Mountain Blossom, chanting for Lobo.

Lobo was already there, with Stone at his side. Lobo wore only moccasin boots and a long white breechclout, with a red bandanna holding his long hair in place and his knife in his hand. He stood at one end of the circle, a slick of sweat on his body. He shifted his weight from one foot to another and waited for Coyotero to appear.

Nearby, Juanita sat with Perico and Peggy, who still hadn't come out of her daze. She stared ahead blankly, her face expressionless, with no will of her own.

Juanita was grinding her teeth nervously, hoping Lobo would win. Perico also hoped Lobo would win, because he hated Coyotero. His mother, White Cloud, sat beside him, praying for Coyotero's death, rocking back and forth.

A cheer went up from the warriors as Coyotero entered the ring. Like Lobo, he wore only a white breechclout and moccasin boots, carrying a knife in his hand, but his headband was blue and white stripes. He was accompanied by several of his loyal warriors, all wearing clothing or trinkets stolen from the McIntyre ranch.

Lobo and Coyotero stood at opposite sides of the circle and stared at each other, their knives in their right hands. Electricity crackled between them, and every member of the tribe knew they were witnessing a momentous event.

Jacinto solemnly raised his hands and clapped them together. "Begin!" he commanded.

Lobo went on the balls of his feet and darted to the side, his hands out, his blade held parallel to the ground, razor-sharp blade up. Coyotero charged across the ring, but it wasn't a blind charge, rather more of a swerving focused charge to the point at which he hoped to collide with Lobo.

It appeared that they'd come together, but at the last moment Lobo jumped back, swinging his knife, and a long red gash appeared on Coyotero's right shoulder. Before Coyotero knew what had happened, blood dripped down his arm and Lobo was nowhere in reach.

Lobo stopped, crouched low, and held his arms out, the blade slanted toward Coyotero, who looked at him for a few moments and then let out a scream, charging across the ring at Lobo.

Lobo didn't move a muscle. He stood poised as Coyotero sped toward him, and then, at the split second before contact, snapped to the side and pivoted, whipping his knife through the air.

Coyotero's scream of triumph became a cry of pain, as a long curved cut appeared across the side of his ribs. His momentum carried him forward and the crowd ran out of his way. He tripped, fell to the ground, tumbled over, and came up on his feet, tensed, waiting for the countercharge, but Lobo was on the other side of the ring, crouched again, waiting.

Coyotero felt pain in his shoulder and side, and clenched his jaw in fury. A raging hatred boiled inside him, and all he wanted to do was cut Lobo to shreds. He walked forward a few steps, then sprang at Lobo again.

Lobo's muscles strained in his arms and legs, and resembled thongs underneath his skin. Coyotero rushed toward him, his teeth bared in rage, and Lobo got low, then dived down at Coyotero's feet, swung his knife, rolled over, and came up on his feet, ready to fight again.

Coyotero's calf was cut deeply from one side to the other, he tripped and fell, bounded around, and landed on his feet again, only this time one foot was streaked with blood.

Coyotero was in deep pain all over his body, but some men fight better when they're hurt the most. He breathed through his teeth and wiped his forehead with the back of his hand. He realized now that he had to settle down and outthink Lobo, otherwise he was going to get killed. He'd already been cut three times, and the fight had only just begun.

He looked at Lobo and realized Lobo simply was too fast for him. The only way to defeat Lobo was to bully and push him around, work him out of position, and cut him down.

Coyotero limped forward, stalking Lobo like a bear who'd been wounded, but was still dangerous. Lobo waited for him, and when he got close danced away.

Coyotero followed him slowly and cautiously, determined not to be faked out again. He had to be persistent and wear Lobo down. It might take all afternoon, but he had to wait for Lobo to make that fatal mistake, while he himself had to remain vigilant, fighting a defensive and offensive fight at the same time.

He plodded after Lobo, and Lobo kept dancing out of the way, turning his body from side to side gracefully, his long hair dancing with his feet, and Stone couldn't help thinking that he looked like a dancer he'd seen perform in Charleston before the war. It had been a troupe from France that was touring America, and Lobo reminded him of the star of the show, who'd been remarkably strong and graceful, and yet there had been the air of deadly menace about him.

Coyotero doggedly followed Lobo around the ring, and the crowd become restless. It was turning into a dance.

Lobo thought he had Coyotero where he wanted him. Coyotero was fighting more cautiously, and all Lobo had to do was slice him up bit by bit.

Lobo shot toward Coyotero suddenly, flicked his wrist,

bounded back, and a lump of flesh a half-inch deep went flying off Coyotero's left shoulder, but Coyotero didn't budge. He'd seen a weakness in Lobo's attack.

Lobo's leg muscles tensed perceptibly a half second before he charged, and Coyotero thought if he could charge at the same instant, his knife would drink Lobo's blood.

Lobo danced to the left, danced to the right, spun out, came back, and then pounced on Coyotero again, but this time Coyotero was ready, lunging forward and ripping with his knife.

Lobo saw the blade coming, and raised his arm to protect his stomach. Coyotero's blade cut into Lobo's left forearm to the bone, and Lobo leapt back, dodged to the side, and took stock of himself.

Blood poured out of his left arm. He tried to move the fingers of his left hand but nothing happened. The hand was useless.

Coyotero was more dangerous than he'd thought, because Coyotero was faster than he'd thought. He looked at Coyotero, who had a faint smile on his face as sweat dripped down his forehead. Coyotero advanced, dragging his wounded leg, blood covering both his arms, but a bright burning fire was in his eyes.

Lobo danced to the side and spun out, but he wasn't so graceful anymore. Pain was in his body and could be clearly seen. He'd lost some of his bounce.

He danced around Coyotero a few times and then suddenly darted in low, snicking his knife through the air, ripping across the top of Coyotero's left thigh, but Coyotero had seen him coming in, and managed to whack the top of his head with his knife.

Both men pulled back from each other, Coyotero bleeding from a deep slit on his thigh, and Lobo from a scalp wound that made the blood flow into his ears and eyes.

Lobo wiped the blood away. At the instant of contact when Coyotero's knife had cut into his head, he'd seen the Ghost Pony. It was only a flash, but it had been there.

He took a deep breath. *It is a good day to die*, he said to himself.

He still had to fight to win. It was the only way for a warrior to proceed, so that his offering would be immaculate.

There was the possibility he could still win. Coyotero was badly cut himself, losing blood too. Maybe the Ghost Pony was for Coyotero, not Lobo. Maybe Lobo was just reading it wrong.

A warrior always had a fighting chance. *Yusn protects the brave*. Lobo stepped forward, holding his right arm out, blade facing Coyotero, who advanced also. The crowd watched breathlessly. Juanita said the Rosary over and over in her mind, going through the Sorrowful Mysteries and the Joyful Mysteries, as she watched the two men in the center of the ring move closer to each other, and the ground beneath them was dotted here and there with red blood.

Lobo tensed, feinted, and darted to the side, dancing smoothly on the balls of his feet. Coyotero altered direction and came after him, lumbering on his two wounded legs. Lobo swooped in, Coyotero charged, and Lobo darted out quickly. Coyotero was off-balance, and Lobo struck again in a movement so fast it was a blur, digging a trench across Coyotero's left side.

Coyotero fell to the ground, rolled over, and was on his knees when Lobo charged again, aiming low to cut Coyotero's face. Coyotero dived at Lobo's ankles, tackled him, and brought him down.

Lobo crashed into the ground, spun around, and raised his arm to grab the wrist of Coyotero's knife hand. Coyotero held Lobo by the throat and choked him, pressing him into the dirt. Then he focused his strength on his right arm and pushed it down toward Lobo.

Lobo's left hand was no good. The Ghost Pony ran in front of him again, and this time there was no doubt about who he was there for.

Lobo knew he had only one chance. Somehow he had to hold Coyotero's knife back, and he pushed with all his strength, but couldn't do it. Coyotero was too strong for him. He saw the Ghost Pony floating before him in the air.

Coyotero growled in his throat like an animal as he squeezed Lobo's throat with one hand and leaned all his weight on his knife, pressing down.

The knife sank toward Lobo's breast, and Lobo looked at it. Lobo and Coyotero vibrated together as they exerted all their strength against each other, but Lobo was clearly losing.

Coyotero was going to kill him, and everybody knew it.

Jacinto sat like a rock, his legs crossed and his hands on his knees. He had interceded to save Lobo last time, but couldn't do it again. One son already was dead, and his only other son was going to be killed by the man he hated most in the world: Coyotero. He closed his eyes, because he didn't want to see the end.

Juanita's eyes goggled out of her head as she watched the knife dip closer to Lobo's chest. She was thinking ahead. They'd make her a slave, but maybe she could escape.

Stone thought about drawing both his Colts and shooting Coyotero, and then fighting for his life against the entire tribe, because that's what he'd have to do if he shot Coyotero. They'd swarm over him in seconds, with knives, hatchets, or anything they could lay their hands on. He relaxed his hands and thought he'd wait and see what happened. If they came for him, he'd defend himself, but wouldn't initiate war against the entire tribe.

He looked at Lobo, whose body was covered with blood and sweat. The knife was only two inches from his chest and it looked as though he was having trouble breathing through his constricted throat that Coyotero throttled with increasing strength every moment.

No smile of victory graced Coyotero's features. His face was contorted with effort, because Lobo was fighting him hard, bringing the strength of his manhood to bear against Coyotero, but it wasn't enough.

Lobo was a warrior to the core. Although his death was assured, he still fought back. A warrior always had a chance as long as he was alive, as long as he fought with all his heart. Surely the mountain spirits would smile on him if he made his sacrifice pure.

The point of the knife was a half inch from his chest. Inexorably it moved closer. Every pair of eyes in the tribe was on the tip of the knife. It touched Lobo's skin just over his heart, and a dot of blood appeared. Lobo strained with all his might, hoping for the warrior's last chance, and the knife bit deeper into his flesh. Lobo took a deep breath and gave it all he had, but the knife pierced more deeply, slipping between his ribs, moving toward the delicate arteries and main organs.

The Ghost Pony walked toward him, its head lowered, and turned to the side. It stood silently, waiting, raising its head up and down slowly. Lobo felt something burst in his chest as blood spurted out around the blade of Coyotero's knife. All Lobo's strength shot out of him in an instant, and he felt himself flying through the air. He landed on the back of the Ghost Pony, who walked forward into the sky.

Lieutenant Lowell rode to the top of the hill and looked down. He saw approximately fifty wickiups facing east in the valley before him, just as the Apache scouts had reported.

His troop was deployed in a skirmish line, their rifles in their hands, ready to attack. The bugler was poised to sound the charge.

It was exactly what he'd been praying for ever since he'd been transferred to the Department of Arizona, and now here it was, lying before him like a gift from God, and the Indians evidently were in the middle of a serious ritual of some kind, not even aware that he and his men were there.

It would be a textbook cavalry charge. The Apaches wouldn't know what hit them. They outnumbered him, but Indians usually broke and ran when attacked in their villages by the U.S. Cavalry.

His men were silent, holding their pistols in their hands, waiting for the order to attack. The gnarled old veterans didn't like the odds, but they were soldiers and had to obey orders. Many of the newer men relished the opportunity to kill Apaches, whom they despised, and they were confident their commanding officer knew what he was doing. A few troopers were scared to death, their teeth rattling in their mouths, and one had a bowel movement while sitting in his saddle.

Antonio sat on his mule and looked down at the village where he'd been beaten and tortured. It looked like too many Apaches to him, and he thought Lieutenant Lowell was crazy. Lieutenant Lowell told him to wait on the hill until the battle was over. Antonio decided he'd flee from the area as soon as it appeared that the gringo soldiers would lose.

Lieutenant Lowell drew his gleaming cavalry saber. He could see the headlines in the Boston papers:

LOWELL DEFEATS APACHES
IN ARIZONA DESERT

All the books said shock and surprise were among the most important elements of the successful cavalry charge. He turned to the bugler.

"Sound the charge!"

The bugler raised his instrument to his lips. The cavalry patrol was poised to strike at the Apache village, where every pair of eyes still was fixed on Coyotero.

With a cry of joy, Coyotero plunged his knife into Lobo's heart, and Lobo went slack on the ground. Coyotero shrieked wildly and stabbed Lobo again in the same place. Then he raised the knife into the air and rammed it into Lobo's throat.

Coyotero looked down at Lobo's corpse. "I have killed you," he said. "I always said I would, and I did."

Coyotero jumped to his feet and raised both his arms in the air. The bloody knife in his hand glinted in the light of the sun.

Jacinto felt sick; his eyes were closed. *I bow to the will of Yusn.*

Coyotero looked over the heads of the crowd and was shocked to see men on horseback lined up on the hill. His jaw dropped open and his eyes were like saucers. "Bluecoats!"

The bugler blew the charge, the sharp staccato notes resounding across the plain. Lieutenant Lowell kicked the ribs of his horse.

The animal galloped down the hill, and the patrol followed. The troopers brandished rifles and shouted battle cries. The charge was on and all they could do was hold on.

They rode into the valley and advanced toward the wickiups, as the Apaches scattered in all directions, except for Coyotero, who stood bloody and battered over Lobo's body. The other Apaches were running for their rifles and pistols, but Coyotero was in no mood to turn his back on his enemy. He had a knife in his hand and the blood of his worst enemy dripping from it. Contemptuous of bluecoats, he was in the mood for fighting.

He narrowed his eyes and searched among the onrushing bluecoats, looking for their leader. If he could kill their leader it would be a great honor, one more on this illustrious day, and it also could take the heart out of the attackers. Coyotero had seen it happen many times. Warriors and bluecoats became confused when their leader was killed.

His eyes picked out Lieutenant Lowell riding in front of the troops, the corporal with the guidon colors to his rear right and the bugler next to him, still playing charge.

Coyotero stepped to the side quickly, to intercept the officer. Twenty horses thundered toward Coyotero, but it didn't faze him.

Stone meanwhile had gathered up Perico, Juanita, and Peggy, and pushed them into the nearest wickiup. He stood outside the entrance and threw his hat away, so the soldiers could see his light hair and know he wasn't an Apache. Then he drew both his Colts and waited to see what would happen next.

An overexcited cavalry trooper might try to shoot him, or maybe an Apache would try to kill him on general principles. He had to be ready. The troopers in blue swept toward him, and it was like the war all over again.

Jacinto emerged from his tent, carrying his Sharps carbine. Majestically he gazed at the onrushing bluecoats, then dropped to one knee and cocked the hammer of his carbine. He took aim down the barrel, and waited for the soldiers to come closer.

Meanwhile, the other Apaches swarmed toward the bluecoats, carrying rifles, pistols, knives, hatchets, and war clubs. The shock of the initial attack had worn off, and now they realized they outnumbered the patrol three to one.

The Apaches dropped to the ground and opened fire at the advancing bluecoats, who leaned around their horses' necks and fired back. Puffs of white smoke arose in the air, and the sound of shots resounded across the mountains.

Captain Danforth held up his hand, signaling for Troop F to stop behind him. He pulled back the reins of his horse, waited until everybody settled down, then wrinkled his brow and listened.

He heard popping in the distance that was unmistakably the sound of battle. Turning to Tim Connors, he said: "I bet that's Lieutenant Lowell!" He raised his right hand in the air, made a fist, and filled his lungs with air. "Troop F!" he bellowed. "Forward at a gallop—hooooooo!"

He spurred his horse, and it raised its front hooves high in the air, then dropped down to the ground and bounded forward. Troop F, with Captain Danforth leading the way, rode hard across the desert, heading for the battle behind the hills straight ahead.

Lieutenant Lowell crouched low in his saddle, holding his saber before him, aiming at the Apaches kneeling or lying all over the valley. They fired furiously at the cavalry, and he could hear bullets whistling all around his head as he thundered toward them across the sand.

An Apache was directly ahead of him, poised on one knee, aiming directly at his horse. *My God*, Lieutenant Lowell thought, *he's going to shoot my horse!* The rifle fired, and Lieutenant Lowell felt his beautiful chestnut roan shudder. He held his sword tightly as the horse crashed toward the ground and tumbled over.

Lieutenant Lowell was thrown clear, and rolled a few times, getting to his feet quickly. He was covered with dust and alkali, his eyes burned, he had to cough, and he saw an Apache with a knife in his hand running at him.

It was Coyotero, who'd stalked him across the battlefield, in a trajectory that brought him directly in front of Lieutenant Lowell. In Lieutenant Lowell's eyes, he looked like the devil incarnate.

Coyotero was covered with blood and moved like a monster, a gory knife in his hand. An expression of extreme malevolence and hatred was in his eyes, and he screamed horribly as he plunged his knife toward Lieutenant Lowell.

Lieutenant Lowell swung his saber the way they'd taught him at West Point, and Coyotero grabbed his wrist, stopping the saber in midair, while stabbing his knife into Lieutenant Lowell's stomach, ripping to the side.

Lieutenant Lowell hollered and fell to the ground, clutching his torn bowels, and Coyotero looked down on him, contempt on his face. This was their leader, and he was only a boy. Coyotero considered it an insult.

The sound of galloping hooves caught his attention. He glanced up and saw a bluecoat riding toward him, aiming a pistol.

The pistol fired, and the bullet exploded into the dirt near Coyotero's feet. Coyotero jumped to the side to get out of the horse's way, then cut in again, leaping up to the bluecoat, wrapping his arms around him, and knocking him out of his saddle.

The bluecoat fell over and dropped to the ground, Coyotero holding him with one hand and raising his knife with the other. Their forward motion caused them to bounce and roll over, as Coyotero struck the soldier again and again with his knife.

Finally they came to a stop. Coyotero got up from him, looked around, and saw a pistol lying on the ground a few feet away. He picked it up and saw another bluecoat on horseback bearing down on him. Raising the pistol, he took aim at the bluecoat.

The bluecoat fired first, and Coyotero sensed the bullet passing his left shoulder. He held steady, aimed carefully at the bluecoat as he passed, and pulled the trigger of his revolver.

It fired and kicked in his hand, and the bluecoat fell off his horse, but his foot was stuck in the stirrup and he was dragged, with a bullet in his heart, into the wickiup area.

The horse and soldier galloped not far from Stone, who stood in front of the wickiup in which he'd placed Juanita, Peggy, and Perico.

For the first time, Stone was the spectator in the middle of a battle, instead of a participant. The main consideration that struck him was that the Apaches significantly outnumbered the cavalry soldiers, and the charge had been ill-conceived. Stone would never have made the charge himself. He didn't like the odds.

The second consideration was that the Apaches were better fighters. They shot the soldiers out of their saddles or leapt on them and stabbed them. Many Apaches shot the soldiers' horses, and then rushed and shot the soldier as he fell to the ground.

Some soldiers managed to shoot Apaches, but the killing ratio was much higher against the soldiers.

What a dumb charge, Stone thought.

The plain was covered with dust and gunsmoke, and Stone couldn't see Sergeant McFeeley's horse get shot out from underneath him. Dazed, with a broken arm and a sprained leg, Sergeant McFeeley got to his feet and aimed his pistol straight ahead at the two Apaches charging him, one with a hatchet, the other with a club.

He pulled the trigger calmly, shot the first Apache, aimed again, and shot the second. Wherever he looked he saw Apaches swarming toward him, jumping over the bodies of fallen troopers.

Sergeant McFeeley knew this would happen to him someday. A soldier can't expect to survive every battle, but soldiering was all he knew. He stood on his one good leg and waited steadfastly for the end.

The Apaches howled and shook their rifles and pistols as they closed in on him. He fired at them but they were quick as jackrabbits, and they aimed shots as they advanced over the bodies of dead horses and soldiers.

His last bullet hit an Apache, who fell to the desert sand, and then he had an empty pistol. Gritting his teeth, sweat pouring down his cheeks, he raised the pistol, to use it as a club, when an Apache in front of him perched on one knee, aimed his rifle, and pulled the trigger.

Sergeant McFeeley heard the explosion and felt a slight pressure on his shirt, and then was dead. He fell to the ground and the Apache who'd shot him jumped to his feet and shouted victoriously.

In the edge of the wickiups closest to the carnage, a tiny figure jumped out of the shadows. He was Perico, who'd escaped from the wickiup behind John Stone. His knife in hand, he thought maybe he could sneak up on a bluecoat and kill him.

He'd watched the battle from behind the wickiups, and it had been fabulous. The warriors from his tribe had destroyed the bluecoats, almost like killing sheep. Perico had seen with his own eyes that Apaches are superior beings. This made him very proud.

All the bluecoats were dead in front of him. Perico advanced toward the nearest one and looked into his face. His face was white and he had a clipped black mustache.

Perico reached into the bluecoat's pockets, wondering what interesting gadgets he had with him, and came out with a gold watch. He looked at it curiously, having never seen one before. Its dial was weird and mysterious. What use could it possibly have? Then he became aware it was ticking. He raised it to his ear, an expression of wonderment on his face.

"What are you doing out here, Perico?"

Perico looked up and saw his grandfather Jacinto walking toward him, carrying a pistol in his hand.

"Look what I've got, Grandfather," Perico said, holding up the watch. "Do you know what it is?"

"It is a machine that tells the white eyes what time of day it is."

"Can't they just look up at the sun?"

"The white eyes are crazy," Jacinto said, taking Perico's hand, walking with him toward his wickiup.

The women and children left the wickiups, slowly at first, looking at dead bodies. Some of the women wailed, seeing a husband or son lying out there among the fallen.

John Stone looked at the desert covered with casualties, and it reminded him of the war. He felt as though he should do something, but there was nothing. This wasn't his fight, unless somebody wanted to make it his fight. He stood with his Colts in his hands, watching the Apaches plundering the battlefield.

Juanita stuck her head out of the wickiup. "Is it over?"

"I believe so."

"Who won?"

"The Apaches."

"Ay Dios!" She came out of the wickiup, placed her hands on his hips, and looked at the battlefield. "What do you think will happen now?"

"I have no idea. Maybe you'd better get back inside that hut, just in case."

Juanita peered ahead and saw a figure hobbling toward her resolutely among the Apaches stealing everything they could find of value on the battlefield. She could feel the Apache's eyes burning into her, and even at that distance recognized him.

"Ay Dios!" she said, and turned around, crawling back into the wickiup.

Stone spotted him coming. With a knife in one hand and a pistol in the other, Coyotero advanced toward Stone across the battlefield.

Stone had been expecting something like this ever since Lobo was killed. He was fair game for anyone in the tribe, but Coyotero would be the most likely assassin.

Stone could respect Lobo, Jacinto, and the other Apache warriors, but he couldn't respect Coyotero, who'd led the slaughter of the McIntyres and killed Lobo, whom Stone had considered a friend. If Coyotero wanted a showdown, he'd get one.

Coyotero saw Stone standing beside the wickiup, a pistol in each hand, and stopped. It could be a long-distance gunfight, but Lobo wanted to fight him man to man, spirit against spirit, and see the expression on his face when the knife went in. Scornfully he threw his pistol onto the ground and raised his knife in the air as he limped toward Stone.

Stone watched him come for a few moments, then dropped his Colts into their holsters. He reached down and pulled the knife out of his boot—it was the one Lobo had given him, with the ten-inch blade sharp as a razor, and the handle made from the thigh bone of a bear.

He walked toward Coyotero, wondering if he was being a fool. *I could shoot him without any trouble,* he thought, but if he did that, the other Apaches might jump all over him. His goal was survival, and it appeared that a knife fight with Coyotero might be the best way.

If he beat Coyotero, he didn't think the other warriors would want to mess with him, but if Coyotero beat him, that would be the end of his road.

He didn't think Coyotero could beat him. He knew Coyotero was a great warrior, but considered himself a first-class fighting man too. He was big, he was strong, he'd been through a lot of hell, and no one had beat him yet.

He and Coyotero trudged toward each other, and pretty soon the Apaches in the area became aware that something was happening. They stopped looting and gathered around Stone and Coyotero, to see the fight.

"Look, Grandfather!"

Jacinto looked up and saw two men walking toward each other, knives in their hands, and although his eyes were bad, he recognized them immediately: the powerfully built Coyotero and tall John Stone with his strange light-colored hair.

Jacinto got to his feet and took Perico's hand. They walked together toward the part of the battlefield where Coyotero and John Stone were converging on each other.

Stone was steady and solid as he made his way toward Coyotero. Stone didn't intend to dance around like Lobo. He'd meet Coyotero head on and go for his jugular.

Coyotero looked more like a beast than a man as he shuffled toward Stone. The muscles were bunched up in his shoulders and a fierce expression was on his face. He'd already killed Lobo and the young chief of the white eyes. Now, to crown his day with glory, he wanted to kill John Stone too.

They came abreast of each other and stopped, staring into each other's eyes. Stone thought Coyotero was a homicidal maniac, and Coyotero saw Stone as the blood brother of his worst enemy. They gripped their knives tightly and went into the knife fighter's crouch.

It was silent. Jacinto sat on the ground ten feet away and stared at the combatants, yearning to see Coyotero bleeding on the ground. If Stone killed Coyotero, Jacinto vowed to give him anything he wanted in the tribe.

Perico stared up at Stone and Coyotero, feeling the energies of their bodies enter his. Something caught his eyes on the horizon of the hills in the distance.

His brown eyes widened, then he pointed and hollered: "Bluecoats!"

Captain Danforth's bugler sounded the charge. Everybody in the valley except Stone and Coyotero turned in the direction of the bluecoats. A huge number of them charged down the hill, three or four times more bluecoats than the last time.

The warriors turned to meet them, now armed with weapons taken from the dead bluecoats on the ground. Women and children ran back to the protection of the wickiups.

"Let me stay with you, Grandfather!" Perico said, drawing his knife. "I will fight them too!"

"Go back to the wickiup!"

"Please let me stay!"

Jacinto smacked the boy in the mouth, but Perico didn't flinch, cry, or show pain. Turning around solemnly, he walked toward the wickiups. Jacinto remained seated, watching Stone and Coyotero. That was more important than the bluecoats.

Captain Danforth rode with his reins in his left hand and his pistol in his right, cocked and ready to fire. The windstream blew back the brim of his hat and the long ends of his rust-colored mustache flew in the breeze.

He led F Troop toward the Apaches, and they saw their brethren in blue lying dead all over the ground. With hatred in their hearts and rifles in their hands, they thundered toward the Apaches.

The Apaches waited, aiming their pistols and rifles at the bluecoats, waiting for them to come closer. They knew they were outnumbered this time, and had to fight harder than ever.

Meanwhile Stone and Coyotero circled each other, holding their knives ready, and Jacinto sat on the ground watching. They heard firing but didn't shift their gazes toward where it was coming from. Stone could see that Coyotero had been slowed down by his wounds, but he'd still be a powerful adversary.

Coyotero knew he had to move fast. The bluecoats were coming, and there were a lot of them. He glanced over Stone's head and was astonished by how many there were.

He had to kill Stone quickly, before those bluecoats saw Coyotero and shot him down. The only thing to do was get in close immediately and start grappling, looking for a soft spot to stick the knife. With a low growl he lunged toward Stone.

Stone darted to the side, but Coyotero changed direction and pounced on him. Stone dodged again, and Coyotero fell on his face. Stone dived on him, raising his blade in the air, ready to jam it into Coyotero's back, but Coyotero spun out and landed on his knees.

Stone was on his knees too. Both men got to their feet as shooting grew louder nearby and the cavalry charge came closer, the ground trembling beneath the pounding hooves of the horses.

Coyotero swung with his knife. Stone leapt back and tried to slash Coyotero's arm with his knife, but Coyotero moved in time and Stone's blade whistled in the wind.

The cavalry came closer. Stone and Coyotero heard shots and smelled gunsmoke as Coyotero edged toward Stone, measured him, and jumped, tearing the air with his knife.

Stone stepped back and thrust his blade at Coyotero's arms, cutting deeply into Coyotero's forearm, but Coyotero backswung with his own knife, ripping Stone across the left biceps.

They stood toe to toe, ripping each other's body, and Stone managed to grab Coyotero's knife hand, while at the same time thrusting his knife toward Coyotero's belly.

Coyotero caught Stone's wrist in his hand, and they were locked together. They held each other tightly and strained with all their strength, noses nearly touching, gritting their teeth. It was a test of sheer strength, and they dug in their heels, pushing against each other, grunting, their faces turning red with effort, trying to drive their knives into each other's chests.

Stone summoned up every ounce of energy he had and pressed it on Coyotero, but couldn't budge him. Coyotero struggled to break Stone's iron tension, but it was like moving a mountain.

Jacinto watched in fascination. Sweat poured down the foreheads of Stone and Coyotero. They sucked wind through clenched teeth and drew the life force from each sinew and fiber in their bodies, but neither could gain an advantage over the other.

A rifle fired nearby, and Coyotero shook as if hit by a bolt of lightning. He looked at Stone quizzically, as blood poured out of his mouth, then his eyes closed. Stone let him go, and Coyotero fell to the ground.

Stone glanced up and saw the U.S. Cavalry in full charge, heading directly for him. He dropped his knife and raised both his hands in the air.

"Don't shoot!" he hollered. "I'm an American!"

No one could hear above the din, and the smoke and dust altered colors and shapes. A bullet whistled past Stone's ear, and he dropped to the ground, looking for somewhere to hide.

The horses galloped past, their riders firing at everything that moved. Jacinto was shot in the chest, and he staggered. He took another step, then lost his balance and fell. Another bullet hit him on the way down.

Stone raised his head and saw the cavalry ride through the village, shooting into the wickiups. He arose and ran toward them.

"Stop shooting! There's children in there!"

A private first class turned his horse around and looked at Stone. He raised his rifle to fire, then became aware of the color of his hair. "It's a white man!" he shouted.

Meanwhile, the rest of the cavalry troop was re-forming for another charge. Captain Danforth turned around and could see only twenty or thirty Apaches still standing, with one of them running toward him, waving his hands, shouting something. A cavalry trooper rode toward this Apache, but then Captain Danforth also noticed the dark blond hair and light skin.

Captain Danforth spurred his horse and trotted toward the American, who continued to wave his hands. The trooper drew close to him.

"What the hell are you doing here?" asked the trooper.

"I'm a prisoner of the Apaches. There are more of us in these wickiups, plus women and children. Who's in charge here?"

"I am," said Captain Danforth, coming abreast of Stone. "Who're you?"

Stone told him his name and how he'd been taken prisoner by the Apaches. "You've got to stop your men from shooting into those wickiups!"

"I'd suggest you find someplace to hide." Captain Danforth turned to his men. "Skirmish line!"

The troop formed long blue lines on both sides of Captain Danforth. They reloaded their pistols and rifles rapidly.

"Bugler, sound the charge!"

The bugler blew the music, and Troop F galloped back across the field, their pistols aimed at the remaining Apaches waiting for them.

Stone watched the troopers sweep forward, and the battlefield became covered with dust and smoke. He couldn't see what was going on, but there was a lot of shooting. The smell of gunsmoke was thick in the air, and occasionally he heard a howl of pain.

He dropped to one knee, took out his bag of tobacco, and rolled himself a cigarette. Lighting it, he took a puff and gazed across the valley.

"San Antone, here I come," he said.

9

COLONEL BRADDOCK MARCHED marched across the parade ground, his campaign hat slanted low over his eyes.

He'd just learned of the massacre at Jacinto's Village. Tim Connors had brought the news, and the first thing Colonel Braddock did was notify Dr. Lantz to prepare for the wounded arriving with Captain Danforth later in the day.

Now he had a more unpleasant task. He was on his way to notify Samantha Lowell that her husband had died bravely in action, fighting the Apaches.

He'd been through this many times in the past, and it was never easy. Most of the women took it well, because they were Army, but occasionally an odd one would pitch a bitch.

Samantha Lowell seemed like that kind of a woman, a little too high-strung, but pretty, with a fine figure. Colonel Braddock wasn't too old to appreciate a fine figure.

He approached the door. The only way to notify the next of kin was just say it straight, be concise, and leave out the bad stuff, such as mutilation.

He knocked on the door and tried to steel himself. He'd rather charge the entire Apache nation with a troop of U.S.

Cavalry than go alone to a woman and notify her that her husband was dead.

The door opened and Samantha stood there, a few of her blond hairs out of place and an uncertain smile on her face at the sight of Colonel Braddock.

"What's wrong?" she asked, a terrible premonition dawning upon her.

"I think you'd better sit down."

He took her by the arm and led her toward the nearest chair. Her heart pounded like a drum and she felt dizzy. She knew what he was going to say, and the walls spun around her. He helped her into the chair. She looked up at him, with the face of an innocent frightened child.

"I'm sorry, Mrs. Lowell," he said, "but I'm afraid your husband, the lieutenant, has been killed in action against the Apaches."

It was a few minutes before midnight, and Stone stood at the bar in La Rosita, raising a glass of whiskey to his lips.

"This one's for you, Sergeant Gerald McFeeley," he said. Hoisting the glass, he slugged it down. "Give me another one," he told the bartender.

A Mexican with a black patch over one eye sat on a chair on the stage and played a dolorous song on his guitar. There weren't many people in La Rosita. Stone looked into his glass and felt rotten.

Too much killing, he thought. *Wherever I go, it seems to follow me.* But deep down he knew it wasn't him. It was the frontier. The frontier was a bloodbath. There were too many people with guns.

He thought of Lobo, as the bartender filled his glass. "This one's for Lobo, a great warrior," Stone muttered, and drank it down.

He remembered the others who'd been with him in the Apache encampment. Peggy McIntyre was being cared for by Colonel Braddock and his wife, until one of Peggy's relatives could be found to take her. She still hadn't said a word and probably would end up in an insane asylum, because of the damned frontier.

Juanita had done better. Captain Danforth took a liking to

her on the ride back to the fort, and the last thing Stone had heard, Captain Danforth had put her up at his own expense at the Cardenas Hotel.

Perico and the handful of other Apaches who'd survived the battle were being taken to the San Carlos Reservation by the cavalry, and it was said to be a terrible place, always hot, lacking water, with no mountains full of game, and the Apaches hated it. When Perico was older, he'd probably leave the reservation and become a warrior, killing cavalry soldiers with the best of them.

The bartender filled Stone's glass, and Stone drank it down. He wiped his mouth with the back of his hand and said: "Do it again."

Stone had been drinking one after the other for two hours straight. There was a heaviness in his body and his eyes were half-closed.

He thought of Lieutenant Lowell, sprawled dead on the battlefield, covered with stab wounds, reeking with gore. Stone had learned that Lieutenant Lowell asked permission to look for him, but found death instead. He'd been a fine young man, but didn't understand his profession. Stone heard he had a young wife. *Bet she isn't feeling so good tonight.*

He raised the glass in the air. "Here's to Lieutenant Lowell," he said, "as fine a young officer as ever was." Then he broke into drunken song:

> "If you want to smell hell, boys,
> join the cavalry . . . "

Stone poured the burning liquid down his throat. The bartender didn't ask if he wanted another one; he just filled the glass to the brim again.

Stone thought about tomorrow. A stagecoach was leaving for El Paso in the morning, and he intended to be on it. He'd be in San Antone by the end of the month.

He took out the picture and looked at Marie. "I hope you're there, kid. We've got a few things to settle."

He tucked the picture back into his pocket and drained his glass. "Hit me again," he said to the bartender.

The bartender filled the glass, and Stone thought of Coyotero, recalling how he and the Apache warrior had tried to cut each other's guts out.

Coyotero had been a formidable opponent. The fight could've gone either way, but strange things happened in battle. The brave man died just as easily as the coward, and much of the killing was random, from stray bullets or blind exploding chunks of steel. Luck counted an awful lot on a battlefield.

Stone raised the glass in the air. "Here's to you, Coyotero," he said. "May you burn forever in hell."

He drank the contents of the glass and slammed it down on the counter. "Whiskey!"

He became aware that the guitar player had stopped. Raising his head, he looked behind the bar and saw the bartender ducking behind the bottles. La Rosita became quiet as a tomb.

Stone pushed his cavalry hat back on his head and turned around to see what was going on. Standing in the doorway, wearing a pistol in a holster, was Antonio Vargas.

Drinkers and gamblers moved out of the way, hiding behind tables and chairs, pressing their backs against the walls. A few ran out the back door.

Stone had drunk too much. He should've been more careful, because he thought Antonio might come looking for him. Riding back to Fort Kimball from the Apache encampment, Antonio had given him numerous dirty looks. But Stone had been tense and needed a drink. One led to another, and now he had to sober up quickly.

Antonio wore new clothes and a big Mexican sombrero. He'd shaved and trimmed his mustache. He took a step toward Stone. "Hello, gringo," he said, holding his hand above his pistol, wiggling his fingers.

Stone stepped away from the bar and faced him. "I had a disagreement with your brother, but I've got no quarrel with you. I think you should let it go."

Antonio shook his head. "There are some things you cannot let go, gringo."

There were some things Stone couldn't let go either. It was going to be gunplay.

Stone's mind became clear. Death was in front of him. He spread his feet apart and planted himself solidly on the floorboards. Slowly, carefully, he raised his hands until they were just above his Colts.

The two men stared at each other. Antonio saw the man who'd killed his brother. Stone saw a young Mexican with a mean look in his eyes. One of them would walk out of La Rosita, and one would be carried out.

"Make your move, if that's what you've got to do," Stone said.

Stone was keyed up, ready to go into action at the slightest movement from Antonio, and Antonio slapped his hand to his pistol, yanking it out of its holster, raising the barrel, and pulling the trigger.

Stone dodged to the side, drawing both his Colts at the same time, taking quick but careful aim, triggering twice.

The silence of the cantina was rent by the explosions of pistols. Stone stood in his crouch and watched Antonio stagger in front of him. Antonio became unstrung, the strength left his body. Dots of blood showed on his new white shirt as he aimed his trembling pistol at Stone for another shot.

Stone fired both his pistols again, and the impact of the bullets rocked Antonio, who took two steps backward, dropped his pistol, and collapsed onto the floor.

Stone holstered his pistols and turned toward the bar, pushing his empty glass forward.

"Whiskey," he said.

WESTERNS!

at least a savings of $3.00 each month below the publishers price. Second, there is never any shipping, handling or other hidden charges—Free home delivery. What's more there is no minimum number of books you must buy, you may return any selection for full credit and you can cancel your subscription at any time. A TRUE VALUE!

Mail the coupon below

To start your subscription and receive 2 FREE WESTERNS, fill out the coupon below and mail it today. We'll send your first shipment which includes 2 FREE BOOKS as soon as we receive it.

Mail To: 1-55773-513
True Value Home Subscription Services, Inc.
P.O. Box 5235
120 Brighton Road
Clifton, New Jersey 07015-5235

YES! I want to start receiving the very best Westerns being published today. Send me my first shipment of 6 Westerns for me to preview FREE for 10 days. If I decide to keep them, I'll pay for just 4 of the books at the low subscriber price of $2.45 each; a total of $9.80 (a $17.70 value). Then each month I'll receive the 6 newest and best Westerns to preview Free for 10 days. If I'm not satisfied I may return them within 10 days and owe nothing. Otherwise I'll be billed at the special low subscriber rate of $2.45 each; a total of $14.70 (at least a $17.70 value) and save $3.00 off the publishers price. There are never any shipping, handling or other hidden charges. I understand I am under no obligation to purchase any number of books and I can cancel my subscription at any time, no questions asked. In any case the 2 FREE books are mine to keep.

Name _____

Address _____ Apt. # _____

City _____ State _____ Zip _____

Telephone # _____

Signature _____
                    (if under 18 parent or guardian must sign)
                Terms and prices subject to change.
    Orders subject to acceptance by True Value Home Subscription Services, Inc.